THE MURDERER
AND THE
FORTUNE TELLER.

THE MURDERER

AND THE

FORTUNE TELLER.

By ALLAN PINKERTON

Black Squirrel Books® 🐿®
an imprint of The Kent State University Press
Kent, Ohio 44242   www.KentStateUniversityPress.com

This facsimile and edition was produced using a scan of a first-edition copy of *The Muderer and the Fortune Teller.* The original edition is part of the Borowitz Collection in the Kent State University Special Collections and Archives and is reproduced with permission.

BLACK SQUIRREL BOOKS® 🐿®
Frisky, industrious black squirrels are a familiar sight on the Kent State University campus and the inspiration for Black Squirrel Books®, a trade imprint of **The Kent State University Press.**
www.KentStateUniversityPress.com

Published by The Kent State University Press, Kent, Ohio 44242
All rights reserved
ISBN 978-1-60635-416-2
Manufactured in the United States of America

First published by W. B. Keen, Cooke & Co., Chicago, 1875.

Cataloging information for this title is available at the Library of Congress.

24 23 22 21 20   5 4 3 2 1

EXPLORING THE
BOROWITZ COLLECTION

Cara Gilgenbach
Special Collections and Archives, Kent State University

The Borowitz Collection, from which the editions of the Pinkerton detective stories are taken, was officially gifted to Kent State University in 1989 by Albert and Helen Borowitz of Cleveland, Ohio. The collection includes primary and secondary sources on crime as well as works of literature based on true crime incidents.

Albert and Helen Borowitz, both scholars themselves, built a scholarly collection—one that affords more than sufficient breadth and depth to support any number of research inquiries. The Borowitz Collection reflects the multidisciplinary expertise of Albert Borowitz (a Harvard graduate with degrees in classics, Chinese regional studies, and law) and his late wife, Helen Osterman Borowitz (a Radcliffe graduate and art historian with literary interests). In addition to collecting, Albert Borowitz is himself a scholar of true crime, having published over a dozen books and many articles on the topic, most notably his masterwork, *Blood and Ink: An International Guide to Fact-Based Crime Literature.*

The Borowitz collection is an extensive one, documenting the history of crime, with primary emphasis on the United States, England, France, and Germany from ancient times to the present day. It includes groups of materials on specific criminal cases that have had notable impacts on art, literature, and social attitudes. This provides the researcher with a wealth of material on those cases and their cultural effects. The collection includes nearly 15,000 volumes of books and periodicals, complemented by archival and manuscript collections. Special areas of note include an excellent collection of Sherlock Holmes and other Arthur Conan Doyle early editions; nonfiction and fiction works related to Jack the Ripper; nineteenth- and twentieth-century British and American crime pamphlets and broadsides; a Wild West collection; crime-related photographs, playbills, postcards, and other ephemera; and artifacts, graphics, and memorabilia related to crime.

The Borowitz Collection includes numerous works of detective stories, both fiction and nonfiction, including books from the Pinkerton Detective Agency series, which embody the collection's central theme, namely how real-life elements of crime infiltrate creative works and works of the imagination. Although true crime is the primary focus of the Borowitz Collection, it also contains notable holdings in several other topics and genres, including a vast collection of sheet music spanning more than two centuries of popular musical taste and distinguished literary collections.

The collection provides rich sources to users as diverse as crime historians, film documentarians, museum curators, television and radio producers, antiquarian book dealers, novelists, and faculty and students of history, American studies, women's studies, and criminal justice, to name just a few. Kent State University is proud to steward this collection, and the present project to republish the Pinkerton detective stories is a further outgrowth of our desire to make these interesting and informative resources available to a wider audience.

CONTENTS.

THE MURDERER

AND THE

FORTUNE TELLER.

CHAPTER I.

ONE sultry day in the summer of 185-, I arrived in Chicago, from a tour I had been making through the Southern States. I had attended to a portion of the accumulated business which I found awaiting me, when a gentleman entered the outer office and asked one of my clerks whether he could see me immediately on some very important business. Mr. Howard saw by the gentleman's appearance, that the matter must be one of great consequence, and, therefore, ushered the visitor into my private office, without asking any questions.

"Mr. Pinkerton, I believe?" said the gentleman, as he advanced toward me.

"Yes, sir," I replied; "what can I do for you?"

He took a letter from his pocket and handed it to me. I motioned him to be seated, while I read the letter. I found it to be from my old friend Chapman, a lawyer in

1

New Haven, Connecticut, introducing the bearer, Captain J. N. Sumner. The letter stated that Captain Sumner was a resident of Springfield, Massachusetts, near which place he owned a farm. He had a moderate fortune, and he was a most estimable man. Mr. Chapman had known him for many years, during which time he had always borne himself in an upright, straightforward manner, free from all reproach. Lately, however, he had become involved in some very serious difficulties in the West, and Mr. Chapman had advised him to see me, and obtain my assistance in extricating himself from his troubles. Mr. Chapman concluded by saying, that he was confident, that, if any one could aid the Captain, I was the best person to consult.

I had not seen Mr. Chapman for some years, the last time having been while I was attending to some business in which he was interested. He was especially noted as a criminal lawyer being employed quite as often for the prosecution, as for the defense. We were the best of friends, and had cracked many a joke at each other's expense. He did not mention the nature of the Captain's troubles in his letters, leaving that for the Captain to do himself.

While I was reading the letter, I was aware that the Captain was observing me closely, as if desirous of reading my very thoughts. When I had finished, I said:

"Captain Sumner, I am glad to meet you. Any one bearing a letter from my old friend Chapman, is welcome."

As I spoke, I looked straight at him, and took in his whole appearance.

He was apparently, about fifty years of age, but was very well preserved, not a streak of gray being visible in his dark, curly hair. He was slightly above the middle height, and his frame was proportionally powerful, his limbs being well knit, and muscular. His clear, hazel eyes looked frankly out beneath heavy, straight eyebrows, while his large Roman nose and massive chin, gave his face great firmness and determination. His teeth were white and regular, and his smile was unusually sweet and expressive. His face was much tanned from long exposure to the weather, and his hands were large and hard. He was dressed in a quiet, neat suit of gray cloth, well fitting but easy, and there was nothing loud or in bad taste about him. His only articles of jewelry were a gold watch and chain, and a seal ring with a peculiar, plain stone, worn on the little finger of his left hand. I gazed steadily at him for about two minutes, which is about as long a time as I need to obtain a correct opinion of a man's character. I was very favorably impressed by his appearance, and I prepared to hear his story with more interest than I should have had, if he had been a less honest, reliable looking man.

He opened the conversation, while I was still looking straight into his face.

"Mr. Pinkerton," he said, "I have heard a great deal about you from various sources, and I little thought that I should ever require your services; but, lately, while consulting Mr. Chapman relative to a possible flaw in the title to my farm, I also laid before him some other troubles which he acknowledged were so serious as to require the advice and assistance of some one with a training and experience somewhat different from his. He urged me so strongly to state my case to you, and obtain your aid, that I have finally decided to follow his advice, and here I am."

"When did you arrive?" I inquired.

"About a week ago. I looked around for a time to see if my difficulties had diminished, ——" (and he passed his hand nervously through his hair, drawing a long breath) — "but I found they had increased, if anything. Mr. Pinkerton, when I retired from the sea and settled down on my farm, I thought my cares and vexations were over, and that I could find in the peace and tranquility of country life, a rich reward for the hardships I had endured while earning enough to retire on. My father, also, was a sailor many years, and, after passing the best part of his life at sea, in like manner, he was able to live his last twenty years in peace and content upon his farm; there I was reared, until I was old enough to go to sea. I have followed his example; but, instead of enjoying the peace he did, I find that my serious troubles are only just beginning. If I were at sea, I should have no fears, for there I am perfectly at home. No matter how the wind might blow, or the seas roll, I always brought my ship through in safety. I could read the signs of the weather, and could detect the approach of danger from the elements. I *knew* my enemies were there, and that was half the battle. Here, on land, I find it so different; my worst enemies come to me with the smiles and greetings of friends; they express the tenderest wishes for my welfare, and shower upon me the tokens of their affection; then, having fairly won my confidence, they turn upon

me when I least expect it, and stab me cruelly. I am a
plain, blunt man — often irritable and unjust, I know —
still, I never flinch from danger when I can see it; but,
the very nature of my bringing up has rendered me unfit
to cope with the wiles and subtleties of my fellow man.
You, Mr. Pinkerton, it is said, have the power to see
direct to the hearts of men through the shams and
artifices by which they seek to hide their true characters,
and you are the only man who can assist me. Oh, I wish
I were back on the sea, far away from all my troubles. I
should care but little if I never returned."

He spoke in a low voice, but the tone was clear until
the last, when his words were very pathetic. As he closed,
his head dropped forward, and he sat gazing fixedly at
his ring in an attitude of mournful retrospection.

"Perhaps you had better wait awhile before telling me
your story," I suggested.

"Yes," he replied, looking at his watch, "it is now five
o'clock, so I will defer making my statement until to-morrow; though I should prefer to make it now, if I had
time. The story is a long one, and I shall have to take a
considerable portion of your valuable time in telling it.
Will you please to name the hour when I can meet you
to-morrow, to give you all the facts in the case?"

I had already become interested in the Captain, and,
after thinking for a moment how I could best arrange my
other business so as to grant him the necessary time, I
told him to come at nine o'clock next morning. He said
he would be punctual in keeping the appointment; then
stepping forward, he took my hand and said, in a very
impressive way, "Mr. Pinkerton, I shall meet you if I am

alive. I am not afraid of death; I have met it scores of times, face to face, and have never flinched from it; but now I must take care of myself. If I don't come, just look for me at my boarding house."

I glanced quickly at him, but could see nothing wrong about his mind. His eyes were clear and natural; his whole appearance showed him to be a plain, blunt seaman, little disposed to invent imaginary dangers. Still, there was in his manner, a deep melancholy, which showed me that it was not any natural disease that he dreaded, and which caused me to exclaim:

"Why, Captain, you fear death by violence, do you not?"

"Yes," he replied; "but I cannot enter into details at present. I shall try to save myself and meet you to-morrow morning, but if I do not come, please send my body to Connecticut, to be interred near the rest of my family."

He then said good-day and went out, leaving me to speculate upon his peculiar behavior, and to wonder what were the dangers which surrounded him. I was so much pleased with his frank, manly simplicity that I was determined to give him all the assistance in my power.

CHAPTER II.

AT nine o'clock the next morning, Captain Sumner walked into my private office, and I immediately locked the door to avoid interruption. I noticed that he was apparently much more contented than he had been the evening previous; but I said nothing, preferring to have him tell his story in his own way. He began immediately, without wasting time in preliminaries:

"Mr. Pinkerton, I know that you are always busy, and that time is money to you; hence, I shall be as brief as possible. In order to begin right, I must go slightly into my family history. My father owned a farm near Springfield, Massachusetts, where my mother brought up the family while he was away at sea. He was as fine a seaman as ever trod a deck, and became Captain in one of the regular lines of East India packet companies while I was a mere child. I had one brother who died very young, leaving me the only boy of the family. I had two sisters, however, Lucy and Annie. My father took me to sea with him when I was quite a boy, and he put me through such a thorough course of seamanship and navigation that, by the time he was ready to resign his captaincy and retire to his farm, I was promoted to the position of first mate in the same line. This was in 1836.

About this time my mother died, and my sisters took charge of the domestic affairs of the farm. My older

7

sister, Lucy, now Mrs. W. R. Lucas, was twenty-two years old. She was a girl of great firmness of character, and she has since proved herself the best of wives, being very domestic and fond of home pleasures. Annie, my younger sister, was eighteen years of age, and she was then my special pride and delight; as, indeed, she has been all her life. She was tall and slender, but well proportioned and graceful. Her features were regular and expressive, and her complexion was very delicate; yet it has retained its freshness until now, instead of fading, as is the case with most clear, soft complexions. She was then, and is still, a beautiful woman. She was very vivacious and witty, was fond of society, and cared less for domestic pursuits than to have a gay time in a large company. She was petted and indulged a great deal, being the youngest and a beauty, so that she was not often called upon to practice self-denial. It is probably partly due to this lack of restraint during her early years that she never has had the strength of character and devotion to good principles as Lucy."

Here the Captain sighed heavily, and stopped speaking for a minute or two. I handed him a glass of ice-water, which he drank mechanically. He then continued:

"As I before stated, I became first mate when my father retired. The company was a wealthy one, owning a number of ships, so that the chances for promotion were very good. My most intimate friend was a young man named Henry Thayer. We had long been ship-mates together, and had passed through a school of navigation at the same time. He was a thorough seaman, a careful, considerate officer, and a true friend. He was a general favorite on account of his cheerful disposition, and we soon became like brothers. Whenever we returned from a voyage, I would bring Henry out to the farm to spend a few days, and, about the time of my promotion, I found that he had become warmly attached to Annie. At every opportunity, he would run down to see her, and in every foreign port we entered, he would be sure to buy some rare and curious present for her. His affection was reciprocated by Annie, and one day, after I had made two or three short voyages as first mate, I returned to the farm and found Annie wearing an engagement ring. I laughingly asked her when it was to come off, and she replied, with many blushes, that they were to be married on Henry's return from his next voyage. I knew that Annie was very fond of gentlemen's society, so I advised her to try to overcome her taste for dress and company; since, when she was married, her husband would be away from home a great deal, and then it would not look well for her to receive much attention in his absence. She seemed to acknowledge the force of my remarks, and said that she should do all in her power to make Henry happy.

"On returning to New York, I found that Henry had been just appointed first mate, and that I had pleased the company so well that they wished me to take command of a new ship which they were building. I gladly accepted the command, and as the ship was not ready for sea, I returned to the farm, where I spent two months. I was somewhat annoyed at Annie's conduct occasionally, as she received, and apparently enjoyed, the attention of several stylish young men, more than was befitting a girl who was engaged to be married. I frequently ran down

8

to New York to oversee the rigging of the new ship, so
that I did not know much about her acquaintances; but
once, on my return, I saw a beautiful amethyst ring on
Annie's finger.

"'Where did you get that ring, Annie?' I asked.

"She laughed gaily and said :

"'Oh! it isn't mine; a gentleman loaned it to me to
wear a few days.'

"My impression was, however, that it had been given
to her, and I feared she was forgetting Henry; so I said:

"'That is a strange way of acting, Annie. You are
engaged to Henry, and you ought to know that it is a
wrong and an insult to him for you to receive a present
from another young man. If Henry knew of this, it
would make trouble.'

"She recognized the truth of what I had said, but she
was determined not to acknowledge that she had done
wrong; so she flew into a passion and said, as sneeringly
as possible :

"'Oh! so you are left here to watch me, are you?
Well, then, just report to him that I can get a better
husband than he is, any day. I am not going to shut
myself up, like a nun in a convent, for any man.'

"I told her that I had no desire to act the part of a
tale-bearer, but that I spoke only for her good; her
conscience must tell her that she was doing wrong. I
concluded by asking her to stay more at home, and thus
prepare for a more domestic life. I did not see the ring
after this, but Annie was very distant in her manner
toward me; her actions showed as plainly as if she had
spoken, that she considered me in the light of an un-

reasonable guardian, who wished to deprive her of all enjoyment. Her giddiness and perverseness caused me much trouble, and I greatly feared she would become reckless after my departure. She was my favorite sister, however, and no matter how she might treat me, I could never lose my love for her.

"The first voyage in my new ship, was a very long one, and, on my return, I found that there had been many changes in my absence. Henry and Annie had been married for sometime, and Henry was then away at sea. As my father had died shortly after the marriage, Annie was living alone in New York, where I called upon her. She was pleasantly situated, and seemed to have everything that could be wished. Lucy was also married, and was living in Morristown, New Jersey. The old homestead had been sold at my father's death, the proceeds being divided between my sisters. A few thousand dollars were left to me, which I deposited in bank with my savings.

"On my return from another long voyage, I was delighted to find Henry at home with Annie, and they seemed more devoted to each other than ever. After this, I saw Henry but twice—once in Singapore, and once in Calcutta. He was then as much in love with Annie, as when he first married her, and he said that she made him perfectly happy. The last time I met him, he had just been notified that he should be given the command of a fine ship on his return to New York; consequently he was in high spirits.

"When I next arrived in New York harbor, I made it my first duty to call on Annie. Much to my surprise, I found that she was teaching music in Brooklyn, at a very high salary. Her musical education had been very thorough, so that she was perfectly competent; but I could not see the necessity for her to teach. She had had one child, but it had died in infancy, and she was living in a fashionable boarding house. I called in the evening, intending to ask her to accompany me for a walk, but she was surrounded by a brilliant company, among whom were several gentlemen, and all were paying her great attention. She was very stylishly dressed, and, to my great disgust, she seemed to be coquetting with several of her admirers. When I was announced, she led me into the library, as if anxious that the company in the parlor should not know that a hard-fisted, weather-beaten sailor like me, was her brother. Still, she spoke very kindly, and seemed glad to see me. She excused herself from going to walk with me on the ground that she had an engagement to accompany the rest of the party to the theatre; but she said that if I would call some other evening, she would gladly go. I was somewhat puzzled by her surroundings and manners, and I determined to have a quiet talk with her as soon as possible.

"The next day, I went to Boston on very important business, and, on my return, I found Annie plunged into all the gayety and dissipation of New York fashionable life. She certainly presented a very elegant and stylish appearance; yet, my heart ached as I looked at her. How much joy it would have given me to have found her in a quiet little home waiting anxiously for Henry's return.

"I talked with her for sometime about her affairs, and urged her to lead a more quiet life; but she insisted that

Henry approved of her present way of living ; of course, I could say nothing further.

" ' Henry is not as unreasonable as you are,' she would say. 'He knew how lonely I would be while he was gone, and, therefore, he told me not to mope and pine, but to get into good society, and try to be cheerful and happy.'

"Still, I had an undefined feeling that Annie was in danger, and I wrote to Lucy about her, asking Lucy to induce her to break away from the gay life she was leading. Soon afterward, I went to sea again, and, during my absence, Henry was given command of one of the finest ships in the line. Two years passed quickly away, but, as I was engaged during that time in making short voyages to the West Indies and back, I frequently saw Annie in New York. She seemed to grow more and more estranged from me, however, and her conduct caused me great anxiety. I had seen some things in her deport-ment, which, though not absolutely wrong, were, to my mind, far from proper ; besides, she showed a carelessness of appearances not at all becoming a married woman.

" My next series of voyages were very long, and I was able to see Annie only once or twice in several years. She was now thirty-two years old, and was unusually and strikingly handsome. About this time, I returned from a long cruise, and found Annie still teaching music in Brooklyn. She dressed as elegantly as ever, and seemed very complacent and contented. I invited her to take a walk with me, and we went out toward one of the small city parks. As she swept along beside me, her features all animation, and her eyes sparkling with health and pleasure, I thought I had never before seen any one so beautiful. I did not wonder that Henry was so proud of her, or that he should indulge her so much. We strolled about in the park for a time, and then seated ourselves in a quiet spot.

"'How long is it since you have heard from Henry?' I asked.

"'Why, don't you know that we had a quarrel several months ago?' she answered, with an effort, her face turning very red.

"'Annie, do you mean that you and Henry have separated?' I asked, very much shocked at such news.

"'Yes; that is what I mean. Henry became so strict and unjust with me that I complained to him of his treatment. One word brought on another, until at last he flew into a violent passion and left me.'

"On hearing Annie relate, in such a cool, off-hand manner, how she had driven away one of the best husbands that ever lived, I was perfectly thunderstruck. I had feared that something of the kind might happen, but now that it had really come to pass, I hardly knew what to do or say.

"'Is it possible, Annie!' I said. 'Where did he go?'

"'I don't know,' she replied; 'he left his ship and went off.'

"'But they know at the office where he went, don't they?' I asked.

"'No; he left his ship at short notice. The company tried to keep him, but he would not stay; and, finally, he went off without telling any one where he was going,' answered Annie, beginning to cry.

"It seemed to me that she was crying more to avert my displeasure than because she missed Henry; but she was my favorite sister, and I still loved her. Hence, though I deeply regretted and condemned her actions, I could not find it in my heart to characterize her conduct as it deserved.

"'Annie, are you not entirely to blame for this? Remember how many times I have cautioned you against the course you were pursuing. Tell me what led to your separation,' I asked, finally.

"At first she refused to say anything; but, at length, I drew out that reports had reached Henry's ears that she was in the habit of accepting a great deal of attention from a certain gentleman, and that he accompanied her to the theatre very frequently.

"'But,' she said, 'there was nothing wrong in that.'

"Then, on several occasions, Henry asked her to attend the theatre with him; but it so happened that she had a severe headache each time. This made Henry jealous, and he asked her, tauntingly, why she never had a headache when a certain gentleman called. This sneer led to mutual recriminations and bitter language on both sides, until Henry went away in a towering rage.

"I could see the whole trouble. Henry loved her passionately, and her conduct had driven him away in despair. I determined to search for him everywhere, in the hope of bringing them again together, and effecting a reconciliation.

"The day before I sailed on my next voyage, I saw a beautiful diamond ring on Annie's finger.

"'Annie,' I asked, sorrowfully, 'whose ring is that?'

"'Why, mine, of course,' she replied; 'have you never seen it before?'

"'You must have plenty of money to be able to buy such valuable jewelry as that,' I said. 'I think you show very bad taste to display it at this time, when you know that your folly has driven your husband from you,' I added, angrily.

"She hung her head in silence, as if really ashamed, and I went away feeling almost guilty for having spoken so harshly to her.

"My next voyage was to the East Indies, and I made inquiries about Henry at every port, besides 'speaking' every vessel I met at sea, but no one could tell me anything about him. It became evident that he had not only left the service of the company, but that he had disappeared from all the localities where he was known.

"On my return to New York, I hurried over to see Annie early in the evening. She was dressed for the opera, and was evidently expecting some one. She was quite surprised to see me, but she threw herself into my arms and kissed me very affectionately, as she inquired whether I had heard any news of her dear Henry. When I told her of my poor success, she pretended to feel very sorry, though she did not apparently allow her sorrow to interfere with her enjoyment.

"'Well, Annie,' I said, 'you are dressed to go out somewhere, aren't you? Tell me all about it.'

"'Yes,' she replied, 'I intended going to the opera with Mr. Pattmore, but if you do not wish me to go, I will remain at home. You must stay to meet him; he is one of the most perfect gentlemen I have ever met.

He belongs in Massachusetts, but he now owns a large hotel in Greenville, Ohio. Mrs. Pattmore and I are *such* good friends, and all the children think the world of me. I have been out to visit them in Greenville twice, and they made my stay so pleasant that I always speak of their house as my home. Mr. Pattmore is in town on business, and I received a note from him this morning asking me to go to the opera.'

"Mr. Pattmore came in just then, and we were introduced to each other. He was a well-built man of about forty-five years of age, with very agreeable, easy manners. His hair and mustache were jet black, and his features were rather pleasing. His eyes were large and black, but restless and snaky; I noticed that he never looked straight into my face when speaking to me. He was dressed in the height of the prevailing fashion, and he showed a good deal of jewelry. They both pressed me to accompany them to the opera, but as I was not appropriately dressed, I declined politely, and they went without me.

"I had previously learned at the office of the company, that they had not heard anything of Henry, so I sorrowfully returned aboard my ship, almost decided to give up a sea-faring life. I was then fifty years of age, and I thought of buying a farm, where I could settle down at my ease. I knew that Annie was in a dangerous position for a handsome woman — left alone with no one to advise or restrain her — and I wished to take her with me, so as to remove her from temptation. I therefore, wrote to Lucy, asking her opinion, and requesting her to advise Annie to give up her present mode of life.

"Lucy wrote a long letter in reply: she said that she very much feared there was something wrong between Annie and Pattmore; when Annie was staying at Greenville, Lucy had written twice, asking her to come to Morristown, where Lucy lived; Annie had promised to do so, but she had never come. Pattmore, Lucy said, was a prominent politician in Greenville, and he was looking forward to the nomination for congressman. Mrs. Pattmore was a very good woman, of fine appearance and agreeable manners; she was very domestic in her tastes and she delighted in taking care of her home and children. There were three children living, the eldest son being about twenty-one years old, and the other two being quite young. Mr. Pattmore's hotel was very well kept and popular, and he was supposed to be wealthy.

"Lucy's letter added greatly to the anxiety which I felt about Annie, and I was very desirous of resigning my command immediately, in order to settle down on a farm with her, and thus remove her from the temptations of a gay city. I felt sure that nothing more would be necessary than a retired, quiet life for a few months, to prepare her to give Henry a joyful and affectionate welcome on his return. Circumstances, however, made it impossible for me to give up my ship at that time, and, at the earnest request of the directors of the company (in which I had invested a considerable portion of my savings) I consented to make one or two more cruises. Accordingly, I sailed for the East Indies for the last time, and made a very speedy and prosperous voyage. I continued my inquiries for Henry Thayer, but was unable to obtain any tidings of him. On my return, I called to see

Annie, and found her occupying her old position as music teacher in Brooklyn. She said that Mrs. Pattmore had urged her so strongly to visit them that she had accepted the invitation twice during my absence.

"I had hardly reached New York, before I was hurried away again; my ship was hastily loaded with a cargo for Rio Janeiro, and I again sailed in command. The trip was a speculative venture, which resulted very profitably, and, on my return, I asked to be relieved from further service. I was then fifty-three years of age, and I needed rest. The company treated me very handsomely, and I sold my shares at a high valuation. Having settled my affairs with the company, I hurried off to see Annie; but I was surprised to find that she had moved to Greenville, where she was teaching music to Mr. Pattmore's younger children.

"I had bought a farm near Springfield, Massachusetts, sometime previous, and, learning that there was some slight inaccuracy in the deed, I went to New Haven to consult a lawyer — your friend, Mr. Chapman — relative to the title. While there, I wrote to Annie, asking her to come and live on the farm with me. She immediately replied that she was under an engagement as teacher for six months, and that she could not leave Greenville until the end of that time. She said that Lucy had asked her to pay a visit to Morristown, but that she had been obliged to decline the invitation for the same reason. In conclusion, Annie begged me to visit her in Greenville.

"As soon, therefore, as I had settled my business affairs, I went to Greenville to stay a few days. Annie seemed very glad to see me, and appeared to be in excellent health. I repeated my proposal, that she should come to keep house for me on my farm, and she seemed favorably disposed toward the arrangement, though she asked time to think about it. I told her that at my death, I should leave her all my property, and that, meantime, she should have everything she wisł ed. I also tried to talk to her about Henry, but she refused to say much, and seemed desirous to believe that he was dead.

"I found that she had very little to do as a teacher, the children being too young to study; but she was much attached to Greenville, as, to use her own words, 'there were so many fashionable people there.' She used to go out driving with Mr. and Mrs. Pattmore, and sometimes with Mr. Pattmore alone, often going as far as fifteen or twenty miles into the country. I did not at all like the way she was acting, and I determined to use every effort to induce her to return to Massachusetts with me. This visit, Mr. Pinkerton, took place about two months ago.

"After remaining in Greenville a few days, I went to visit Lucy in Morristown. We had a long talk together about Annie, and finally, Lucy confided to me that she feared that Annie was *enceinte*.

"'Good heavens, Lucy! that is impossible!' I exclaimed. 'Our family has never had such a disgrace cast upon it before; it has always maintained its purity. No, no; it can't be possible.'

"'I am not *sure* of it,' said Lucy; 'but I know there is something wrong with her, and I greatly fear that she is a ruined woman.'

"I hardly knew what to say or do, the mere suspicion was such a terrible blow."

Here the Captain became greatly affected; the perspiration started on his forehead in large beads, and he often made long pauses, as he continued. His emotion would sometimes entirely overcome him, so that he could not speak.

"Well," he went on, "Lucy wrote to Annie, and back came the answer fully confirming the horrid suspicion. Annie freely confessed that she was *enceinte*, and that Pattmore was the father of her unborn child. She said that she and Pattmore dearly loved each other, and that she could not bear the thought of separating from him.

"My first impulse was to curse her and never see her again; but my old love for her could not be set aside, and pity soon took the place of anger. I could see that Pattmore had thrown a spell around her by his fascinating manners, and she was completely under his influence. I determined to save her from exposure and disgrace, if possible, and, therefore, started for Greenville immediately. I had intended to speak to Annie in a severe and indignant tone, but she rushed to meet me with such a glad little cry that my anger melted away, and tears sprang unbidden to my eyes.

"'Oh! Annie! Annie!' I exclaimed, 'what have you done! How has this man acquired such a terrible power over you as to make you forget your marriage vows and live a life of infamy with him? Have you no stings of conscience? Think how our sainted mother would feel if she could see her little Annie in the power of a heartless libertine. Return with me at once, and I will forget everything. In the seclusion of my farm, you need not fear the fiery tongue of scandal, and I will be a father to your child.'

"She stood with downcast eyes while I was speaking, but when I had finished she began a vehement defense of her conduct, in the course of which she repeated all the usual arguments of those who wish to ease their consciences when on the downward path.

"Mr. Pattmore, she said, was a perfect gentleman; he loved her, and she returned his affection; it was true, unhappily, that they were both married, but nature had intended them for each other, and she preferred to obey the laws of nature to those of society; Mrs. Pattmore was a very fine woman, but she could not make her husband happy.

"The doctrine of free-love was fully endorsed by Annie, who had learned it all by heart, and she advanced the most extraordinary theories in justification of her conduct.

"For years, she said, she had held the first place in Pattmore's heart, and he had lavished his money upon her freely; the diamond ring I had seen, the rich dresses she had worn, a valuable necklace, and many other articles of jewelry were among the gifts he had showered upon her; they loved each other as husband and wife, and as soon as Mrs. Pattmore should die, Mr. Pattmore would make Annie his legal wife.

"I saw that she was completely infatuated, but I endeavored to show her how false her reasoning was, and to what wicked conclusions it would lead. I asked if she had forgotten Henry, who was liable to return at any moment; she could not marry until she obtained a divorce. Besides, the fact that they were looking forward to, and wishing for Mrs. Pattmore's death, was almost equivalent to committing murder, since to desire any person's death was morally as bad as to murder that person.

"We had a long conversation, and finally Annie agreed to join me in Springfield in a short time. I therefore returned to the farm and prepared to settle down. I received no reply to several letters which I wrote to Annie, but. at last she sent me a short note saying that she had changed her mind, and that she should stay in Greenville. I immediately replied that I would not permit her to remain there any longer, and I then went to consult Mr. Chapman about the matter. He acknowledged that he could do nothing, as Annie was her own mistress; but he advised me to see you, Mr. Pinkerton, and obtain your advice and assistance. As it was a very delicate matter, affecting the honor of my family, I did not like to speak about it to a third party, as I feared that the story might be made known publicly, and Annie's reputation would then be ruined. I therefore told him that I should not consult you if I could possibly avoid doing so.

"While I was inwardly debating what was best to be done, I received a note from Annie, asking me to come to her, as she feared that something serious was about to happen. I went at once to Greenville, and found that she had decided to remove the evidence of her guilt by performing an abortion. I tried hard to dissuade her from a step which might result in her own death, but she was resolute in her determination not to wait for the child's natural birth. She said that if I would stay with her until she recovered, she would return to Springfield with me and never see Pattmore again. She spoke very feelingly about Henry, and she seemed so deeply and truly penitent that I was finally won over to her wishes, and I agreed to stay with her until she had an operation performed. I determined to take her to stay with Lucy, at Morristown, at first, and she accordingly prepared to leave Greenville.

"She had a long private interview with Pattmore before leaving, and when she came out I saw she had been shedding bitter tears. As I stepped to the office desk to pay my bill, I saw Pattmore in the clerk's room back of the office, and he, too, seemed very much dejected. I could hardly keep my hands off his throat when I recollected his villainy ; but I curbed my temper by a great effort, as I knew that a personal encounter between us would only publish my sister's shame to the world. On our arrival in Morristown, Lucy and I had a long talk with Annie, which was far from satisfactory to me, as I saw that she was still infatuated with Pattmore.

"I thought best to go some distance away from the places where we were known during Annie's trial, and I therefore brought her to Chicago. Here I obtained board in a very respectable family, where there were only a few other boarders. Annie did not show her condition in her appearance at all, and no one could possibly have suspected her. I found a physician named Enfield, who was a noted operator in such cases, and Annie at once placed herself under his treatment.

"I knew that I was about to assist in committing a

great crime, yet I felt that I must shield Annie at all hazards, and so I yielded to her wishes in the matter. Enfield was an expert in such matters, and, in a short time, he brought Annie through in safety. She was recovering fast, when one day, on entering her room, I found Pattmore there. I went out instantly, as I was afraid to trust myself in the same room with him; but, when he had gone away, I besought Annie never again to admit him to her presence. She would make no promises, and finally, she fell back in a swoon. On recovering, she said that she would die if she could not see Pattmore, and I was obliged to drop the subject until she should become stronger. Pattmore remained in town two days, and she insisted on having him with her a great deal of the time.

"I fear that you will consider me very weak and foolish for permitting this; but I have never been able to refuse Annie anything. I knew, moreover, that, in such a case, harsh measures would only add fuel to the flame, and so I continued to humor her, trusting, that in time, she would gradually recover her normal condition, and see the folly of her conduct.

"Pattmore told her, during his visit, that he was in great hopes of receiving the democratic nomination to Congress; and, as the democratic party had a large majority in that district, the nomination would be equivalent to an election. He also said that his wife was in failing health, and that she seemed to grow weaker every day. I could see by Annie's manner, when she told me this, that she hoped to be Pattmore's partner in

9

enjoying the gay life of the National Capital, though she did not say so directly.

"One day, she brought up the subject of wills, and said that she thought every one owning property, ought to make a will. She said that otherwise a man's property, in case of sudden death, might be eaten up by the lawyers and court officials. I admitted the justness of her remarks, and told her that I should follow her suggestion. I was obliged to go East on business for a few days at this time, and, on the way, I left a letter and package with Pattmore, which Annie had asked me to deliver. While in New Haven, I employed Mr. Chapman to draw up my will. Lucy had asked me to leave all my property to Annie, as she had enough for herself and children, while Annie had no one to look to for an honest support, except myself; accordingly, I made my will in that way.

"On my return to Chicago, I hurried to our boarding house to see Annie, and, to my intense disgust, I found Pattmore with her. The sight of him fondling my poor sister, was too much for me: and, although I succeeded in restraining myself from doing him any personal violence, I used the most severe language possible in characterizing his villainy, and in expressing my contempt for him. I concluded, by telling him that the affair must end then and there; that he must never address my sister again, or attempt to see her; and that if he dared to disregard my demand, he must take the consequences. They both hung their heads guiltily, while I was speaking, and when I closed, Pattmore quitted the room without a word. I found that he left town the same day.

"I also went out of the house immediately, being too

excited to talk calmly to Annie; but I returned after
supper, and reasoned with her as gently as possible on
the impropriety and wickedness of her conduct. She
seemed to feel very sorry, and was so penitent that my
hopes of saving her, rose considerably. She promised,
with tears in her eyes, to overcome her unholy love for
Pattmore, and never to see him again. I noticed, however,
that when I spoke of my efforts to obtain tidings of
Henry, she was very indifferent; but she promised to
return to Springfield with me as soon as she was able to
travel, and matters began to look more cheerful for the
future.

"A day or two after, she received a letter from Pattmore,
saying that his wife was seriously ill, and that the physi-
cians considered her life in danger.

"'What is the matter with her?' I asked.

"'I don't know,' she replied; 'Mr. Pattmore does not
state what is her disease.'

"I then spoke very harshly about Pattmore, and said
that he, above all other men, was hateful to me, because
he had ruined her. She replied in his defense, and, as
our conversation seemed likely to become bitter, I walked
out to allow time for both our tempers to cool off. On
my return, I found that Annie had gone out for the first
time, since her illness, but she soon came in, saying that
she had taken a short walk for exercise. She had regained
her good humor, and seemed more like herself than she
had for sometime. She again brought up the subject of
wills, and I told her that I had made my will while I was
in New Haven. She asked me about it, and I told her
that I had made her my sole legatee, and that she would

be in comfortable circumstances when I died. She seemed very much pleased at this, and said I was a dear good brother; but she hoped it might be a long time before she should become heiress to my property.

"'Who knows?' she said, laughing; 'perhaps I may die first.'

"'That is possible,' I said, 'but not probable. In the course of nature, I ought to die many years before you; and sailors are proverbially short-lived.'

"'Oh, nonsense!' she replied, 'you are so salted and tanned that you will last fifty years yet.'

"She then skipped gaily into the next room and brought out a bottle of ale, to reward me, as she said, for being good. She poured out a glass for each of us, and we drank to each other's good health. In about half an hour I became very sick; I vomited and retched terribly, while my bowels seemed to be on fire. The weather was very warm, and I attributed my illness to some fruit I had eaten, which the ale had disagreed with. I suffered agony all night, but toward morning I became quieter and the pain gradually left me.

"At daylight I casually glanced at my ring, and I was surprised to see that the stone had turned to a creamy white—a sure sign that my life was in danger. You will call me foolish and superstitious, I know, but I cannot help it. A belief in the virtues of this ring is a part of my very nature, and it has always been an unerring guide to me. This ring invariably predicts my good or bad fortune." And so speaking, the Captain held the ring out for me to see it.

I looked him straight in the face, expecting to see some

"And so speaking, the Captain held the ring out for me to see it."

signs of insanity, or at least monomania, in his eyes, but there were none. He was evidently perfectly rational, and this belief was apparently as natural to him as a belief in a hereafter, or in any other religious doctrine, is to other people. After a short pause, as I glanced at the ring, he continued:

"Now, you can see nothing strange in that stone, Mr. Pinkerton, but I can. From its appearance I can obtain warning of approaching good or bad fortune. Away out at sea, when a storm is coming, the stone turns black; when enemies are near me it turns the color of blood; and when I am in danger of death, it becomes a creamy white.

"My father once saved the life of a Sepoy soldier, and, as a mark of gratitude, the latter presented my father with three rings of wonderful powers. The Sepoy said that he had obtained them from a Hindoo hermit, far out in the jungle. I have long tried to find other rings possessing the same qualities, but have never succeeded. One of these rings was buried with my mother, one with my father, and I have the third."

I looked at the ring carefully, but could see nothing remarkable about it. The stone was an opal, set in a heavy gold band, peculiarly chased; but, aside from the popular superstition with regard to opals, there was nothing which would lead me to suppose that it possessed any exceptional powers.

"When I saw you last," continued the Captain, "I meant to have asked you to have this ring buried with me, in case I died; but I was afraid you would consider the request too foolish. I wished it buried with me because I did not wish Annie to have it."

"But why do you think Annie would take it?" I asked.

"Because I know she wants it," replied Captain Sumner. "She thinks that it would enable her to make Pattmore love her always, and so she wishes to own it. Now, I think Pattmore is a villain, and I wish to separate her from him and destroy his influence over her. Therefore I do not wish her to get the ring, since its possession will induce her to continue her connection with that man."

I confess that I did not know what to make of the Captain. If he was insane, he certainly had the most impenetrable mask over his insanity that I had ever seen. His eyes were so bright, clear and honest, that the most experienced physiognomist in the world would have failed to observe the slightest trace of cunning, or want of a balanced mind in their expression. During the progress of his story he had continually held his ring where he could see it, and several times had raised it to the light, in a contemplative sort of way, as if he drew some satisfaction from its appearance. He bowed his head in his hands as he ceased speaking, and some moments elapsed before he looked up, though when he did so he was perfectly calm.

"Captain, did you find the ring of any practical value at sea?" I asked.

"Yes; often it has apprised me of a coming storm in time to prepare for it. I have thus passed in safety through many sudden gales of the approach of which I have been warned only just in time to save my ship.

My men always had perfect confidence in my ability to weather the heaviest gale."

"Well, Captain, if you should give that ring to me, would it be equally prophetic in my hands?" I asked.

"But I will not give it to you nor any one else; nor will I part with it, even in death if I can help it," replied the Captain. "The Sepoy told my father, that he must never allow the rings to go out of his family, as they would then lose their powers. I know that the fancy seems strange to you, and, no doubt, you think I am not exactly sane; but I have proved the power of the ring so often, that I know its virtues, and believe in them. I may be able to satisfy you of its value by a practical demonstration yet."

I saw that he was not insane, but terribly superstitious, so I made no further remarks about the ring. He drew his chair closer toward me, and said in a low, painful whisper:

"Mr. Pinkerton, I have positive knowledge that *Annie has attempted to poison me three times.* She put poison in that ale; she afterwards gave me some in a cup of coffee; and, the third time, it was administered so secretly, that I do not know when I took it. The first time, I recovered because the dose was too large, and I vomited up the poison so soon that it had not time to act. The second time, I took only a sip of the coffee, and found that it tasted bitter, so I threw it away, though the little I had taken distressed me exceedingly. The third time, I nearly died, and it was only by the prompt attendance of a physician that I was saved. He said it was a metal poison which probably came off from a copper kettle in which some fruit had been cooked. Neither he, nor any one else, ever suspected that I had been poisoned intentionally. When I recovered, I accused Annie of trying to poison me; she denied it vehemently at first, but I said to her:

"'Annie, the ring tells me that I have an enemy near me, and you must be that enemy.'

"I spoke as if positive of her guilt, and, as she is a firm believer in the ring, she finally burst into tears and confessed having given me poison at three different times. On her knees, she begged my forgiveness, and thanked God that my life had been spared. She was so broken down by the thought of her unnatural and wicked purpose, that I feared that she would have a relapse into sickness. She seemed so wholly contrite, that I thought she would never undertake such a terrible crime again, and I freely forgave her."

I looked at the Captain in perfect amazement, hardly able to credit my own senses.

"Can it be possible," I asked, "that your sister admitted that she had tried to poison you?"

"Yes," replied the Captain; "and she said that Pattmore had encouraged her to put me out of the way. He had told her that he would marry her when his wife, (who was now dying) was dead; that I was bitterly opposed to him, and would never consent to their marriage; that if she would poison me, they would be married and go to California to live; and, therefore, that it would be well for her to poison me before Mrs. Pattmore died."

"What!" I exclaimed, "is Mrs. Pattmore dying? What is her disease?"

"I do not know," replied the Captain; "but I fear that *she, also, has been poisoned.*"

"How long is it since you had this talk with Annie?" I inquired.

"About three days ago, and she has been sick abed with excitement and remorse ever since. She says that she expects to hear of Mrs. Pattmore's death at any time, and she is sure that Pattmore has poisoned her. Mr. Chapman told me, when I last saw him, Mr. Pinkerton, that you were the only person who could help me; and so I have come to you to save Mrs. Pattmore and my sister. I feel that Mr. Chapman was right, Mr. Pinkerton, and I beg you to give me your assistance — I will pay you liberally."

CHAPTER III.

WHEN the Captain had finished his almost incredible story, I hardly knew what to make of it. It was impossible to doubt his word; yet it seemed almost equally hard to believe that his sister could have tried to murder him. Pattmore's intention of killing his wife in order to marry Annie, was another piece of cold-blooded villainy which was almost past belief. The question frequently came into my mind: Are all the parties in their right minds? After I had thought about the matter in silence a few minutes, I said:

"Well, Captain Sumner, yours is certainly a strange case, and I cannot give you any answer until I have had time for reflection. Return in three hours and I will then tell you my decision. I will help you if I possibly can do so."

He rose to go, but stopped a moment as he reached the door, and said, with the utmost simplicity and confidence:

"I *know* you can help me if you will do so, and no one else can."

After he had gone, I sent a man to the Captain's boarding house with instructions to learn all he could about the boarders. He reported that, among others, there was a Captain Sumner boarding there with his sister, Mrs. Annie Thayer. My detective also learned many things about the Captain and his sister which cor-

roborated the account given by the Captain.   Having
satisfied myself that the Captain's story was true—in part
at least—I sat down to reflect upon the strange medley
which he had told me.

Mrs. Thayer had, undoubtedly, committed a serious
crime against her husband, besides making the attempt
on her brother's life; but I could not have her punished,
for her brother's object was to save her from the ruin in
which her downward course would probably end.   Pattmore, however, was a dangerous man, and it would be
necessary to proceed with caution in handling him.   He
seemed to be a villain at heart, and it was probable that
he only sought Mrs. Thayer's society in order to gratify
his sensual passions.   Perhaps the Captain's suspicion,
that Mrs. Pattmore's illness was caused by poison administered by her husband, was correct; if so, it would be
necessary to act at once, before she should become his
victim.   It was barely possible that he might intend to
get a divorce from his wife and then marry Annie; but I
did not consider this supposition a very probable one.
He wished to be elected to Congress, and he would not
dare to give such an opportunity for scandal as would
ensue if he attempted that course.   No; poison had
been his reliance in one case, and he would not scruple
to make use of it again.   Mrs. Thayer was probably well
informed as to all his plans, but, evidently, she would not
willingly divulge anything prejudicial to her lover.   Her
brother was clearly unable to compel her to confess
anything, or he would not have applied to me.   Moreover he could refuse her nothing, and he would certainly
object to any attempt to force her to give evidence

against her will. He admitted that she was weak, vain and thoughtless; that she had been false to her husband; and that Pattmore had completely bewitched her; yet the Captain resolutely stood between her and harm.

She could tell all of Pattmore's secrets if she were so disposed, and it would be easier to get information out of her than out of him; the question was—how shall I go about it?

I reflected that she was very superstitious, as shown by her belief in the Captain's ring; it occurred to me that I might take advantage of that trait of her character to draw her secrets out. Why could I not introduce a fortune-teller to her, and thus learn all I wished to know? The idea seemed to me to be admirably adapted to the necessities of the case. I sketched out, in my mind, a skeleton plan of operations about as follows:

I should entrust the case to one of my female detectives; she would be posted upon all the points of Mrs. Thayer's history; she would be required to learn enough of astrology, clairvoyance and mesmerism, to pass for one of the genuine tribe; the plan would be so arranged that Mrs. Thayer would voluntarily consult this fortune-teller, who would soon gain a complete ascendency over her superstitious nature by revealing to her all her past life; finally Mrs. Thayer could be brought to tell all she knew of Pattmore as a means of aiding the sibyl to read her future.

This plan seemed to me the most feasible of any, and I therefore decided to adopt it in working up the case against Pattmore. After all, he would be the one against whom my efforts would be directed, Mrs. Thayer being only an unconscious instrument in bringing him to justice. In case it could be shown that he had actually attempted to murder his wife, I was determined that he should not escape the swift vengeance of the law.

Just as I had concluded my deliberations, the Captain hurried into my office, the perspiration standing in great beads on his forehead.

"Mr. Pinkerton, I fear we are too late!" he exclaimed in a husky voice. "Annie has just received a telegram from Mr. Pattmore, saying that his wife is dead."

"*Dead!*" I repeated. "Is it possible! When did she die?"

"To-day," he replied.

"It will be an easy matter to discover the cause of her death," I said, after a moment's pause. "We must have a *post mortem* examination held."

"That may be possible," replied the Captain; "but you must recollect that Pattmore has a great many friends in Greenville; that, in fact, he is a prominent candidate for the Democratic Congressional nomination; and, even if he were supposed to be guilty, the party would make a strong fight to protect him, as they could not afford to have him exposed."

"Is it possible that he has so much influence as that?" I asked.

"Oh, yes," said the Captain; "he is a brilliant speaker, and a very agreeable man socially, so that he makes many friends. He is such a wily scoundrel that I fear we shall have great difficulty in tracing any crime directly to him. I do not care whether he is convicted or not, provided I can rescue Annie from his clutches. He has apparently cast a spell over her, and she is wholly controlled by him."

"If that is the fact, we must use strategy, and undermine his plot with a deeper one. I will accept a retainer from you, Captain, and then we will proceed to work up the case."

The financial part of the arrangement having been adjusted, I gave the Captain some advice as to what he should do. I told him that he must place implicit confidence in me, and not try to interfere in any manner with my plans. If he could not do this, I should withdraw at once. He must come in to see me often and keep me well informed; but he must not expect me to tell him about my plans, any further than I should see fit. I should try to show Pattmore's villainous character to Annie, and if I could gather sufficient evidence that he had poisoned his wife, I should bring him to justice. I then told the Captain that he ought to have a quarrel with Annie, at the end of which he should burn his will in her presence, and leave her; on going out, he should tell her that he intended immediately to deposit his ready money in bank, and make a will wholly in favor of Lucy. This would prevent Annie from again attempting his life, as she would have nothing to gain by his death.

The Captain was satisfied to accept my conditions, and he said that he had full confidence in my ability. All that he desired was to save Annie from the power of Pattmore, and from the ruin which would inevitably result from their further intercourse. He then went home to have his quarrel with his sister.

I determined to send a detective named Miller, to

Greenville, to obtain board at the Pattmore House, and, if possible, to become intimate with the proprietor. This part of my plan would require prompt action, as Pattmore might succeed in removing all evidences of his guilt. I therefore, sent for Mr. Miller, and went over all the facts of the case with him, giving him full instructions as to his duties. He was to hail from Bangor, Maine, and to represent that he wished to start in the lumber business in Greenville, if the prospects were good. I told him to post himself thoroughly upon the qualities and prices of all kinds of lumber, lath, shingles, etc., and to read up the local history of Bangor. To make matters easier for him, I gave him a letter of introduction to a lumber dealer in Greenville, with whom I was well acquainted. The next day, Miller was ready, and he took passage to Buffalo by steamer, going thence to Greenville by rail. He then took a room at the Pattmore House, and soon became acquainted with the proprietor.

The same day that I gave Miller his instructions, I sent for Miss Seaton, one of the detectives in the female department, and ordered her to make arrangements to take board in the same house with Captain Sumner and Mrs. Thayer. Miss Seaton was a brunette, about twenty-seven years of age; she was of agreeable appearance and pleasing manners; she had been a school teacher, and was a good judge of human nature. Mrs. Warne, the superintendent of the female department, said that Miss Seaton was very sharp, and that nothing could escape her piercing black eye. She was to cultivate Mrs. Thayer's acquaintance, and endeavor to win her confidence. This would probably be a difficult task; but I told Miss Seaton to be patient and discreet, and not to be discouraged, if she should not be immediately successful. By pretending to be in poor health, she could obtain Mrs. Thayer's sympathy, and their progress toward intimacy would be accelerated. Miss Seaton immediately moved to the City Hotel, whence she set out to look for a boarding place. By a curious coincidence, she could not satisfy herself until she came to the house where Mrs. Thayer was boarding on the North side. There she found a pleasant room adjoining Mrs. Thayer's, and it suited her exactly. That evening at supper, she was introduced to her fellow boarders, of whom there were only three besides the Captain and his sister.

The employment of female detectives has been the subject of some adverse criticism by persons who think that women should not engage in such a dangerous calling. It has been claimed that the work is unwomanly; that it is only performed by abandoned women; and that no respectable woman who becomes a detective can remain virtuous. To these theories, which I regret to say are quite prevalent, I enter a positive denial. My experience of twenty years with lady operatives is worth something, and I have no hesitation in saying that the profession of a detective, for a lady possessing the requisite characteristics, is as useful and honorable employment as can be found in any walk of life.

Previous to the early part of 1855, I had never regularly employed any female detectives; nor were women engaged in that capacity in any part of the Union. My first experience with them was due to Mrs. Kate Warne, an intelligent, brilliant, and accomplished lady. She offered her services to me in the early spring of that year, and, in spite of the novelty of her proposition, I determined to give her a trial. She soon showed such tact, readiness of resource, ability to read character, intuitive perception of motives, and rare discretion, that I created a female department in the agency, and made Mrs. Warne the superintendent thereof.

The work of my female detectives is generally light. Zeal and discretion are the principal requisites, though conscientious devotion to duty, and rigid obedience to orders, are also essential. They are expected to win the confidence of those from whom information is desired, and to lose no opportunity of encouraging them to talk about themselves.

With regard to the moral influence of their duties, I say boldly that it is in no respect different from that of any other position where women are thrown upon their own resources. It is an unfortunate fact in our social system, that no single woman or widow, dependent upon herself for support, can escape a loss of caste and position by working in the great field of business where she comes in competition and contact with men; but, aside from this general prejudice, there is nothing in the detective's duties to make her profession less respectable and honorable than there is in the duties of a lady cashier, book-keeper, copyist, or clerk. The detective's temptations are no greater than those of any of the foregoing who mingle with men in their daily business; while, on the other hand, the safeguards of their virtue are much more numerous, since all the detectives of my agency know that their conduct is under constant surveillance.

10

There are instances of frequent occurrence where great criminals are successful in hiding all traces of their guilt so effectually as to make their conviction impossible without the aid of the female detective. Most of these men have wives or mistresses in whom they confide to a great extent. The testimony of these women, then, become the sole means by which to convict the criminals, and their testimony can be obtained in only one way—a female detective makes their acquaintance, wins their confidence, and draws out the story of the crime. Such an instance is given in "The Expressman and the Detective," hitherto published.

I have in my employ several ladies of unquestionable purity of life, who are also among the most successful operators on my whole force. I take pleasure in offering this tribute to their ability, and their spotless characters.

The next day the Captain called to see me, and said that, according to my advice, he had quarreled with Annie about Pattmore, and had worked himself into a great rage. Finally, he had torn up and burned his will, saying that he should immediately make another, leaving everything to Lucy.

"So far, so good," said I; "she now will have no motive for poisoning you, so you can rest in peace."

The Captain stated further that he had deposited in bank a few hundred dollars which he had brought with him, so that he felt comparatively safe for the present.

That evening Miss Seaton reported that Mrs. Thayer had left the house shortly after the Captain. Miss Seaton had followed her to the post-office, where Mrs. Thayer had deposited a letter, and had received another at the ladies' window. She had immediately torn it open, read it hastily, and crumpled it in her hand, while slowly walking home. I was very anxious to know to whom she had written, and also who had written to her. I immediately 'wrote to Miller to watch Pattmore's mail, and to learn whether there were any letters in it from Chicago. If so, I wished him to obtain a view of the handwriting, and, if possible, to get possession of the letters themselves long enough to take copies of them.

The next morning Captain Sumner came in again, but he had nothing to report.

"Does Annie write much?" I asked.

"No, very little," he replied.

"Does she correspond with Lucy?"

"Sometimes, but not regularly."

"Did she not write a letter two days ago?" I inquired.

"No," answered the Captain; "but why do you ask?"

"Oh! for no particular reason; however I wish you would write to Lucy and inquire whether she has received a letter from Annie lately; also whether she has written to Annie."

"Certainly, I will do so now," said the Captain, and, he straightway sat down to write to Lucy.

In a few days, the Captain received a letter from Lucy stating that no letters had passed between her and Annie for over a month. This made it certain that Lucy was not Annie's correspondent.

Miller sent in a report about the same time, saying that he had become slightly acquainted with Pattmore, who was deeply mourning the death of his wife. Even the mere mention of her name was sufficient to draw tears to his eyes, and her loss had so severely affected him that his friends were afraid he would never be the same man that he had been during her life.

Miller had expressed an intention of opening an office in Greenville, and Pattmore had given him some valuable advice and information relative to the lumber market in the interior. Since getting my letter, Miller had noticed that Pattmore had received four letters from Chicago. Miller said that he had not been able to obtain possession of these letters, but he should make a great effort to capture those which might come in the future. He had taken pains to cultivate the friendship of the clerk of the hotel, and he was on such good terms with him as to find it convenient to pass a great deal of time in the office. He had noticed that when the clerk received the mail, all of Pattmore's letters were put into a particular box behind the desk, and he hoped to be able to secure some of them.

I had devoted a large amount of thought to this singular case, and I finally decided that I would go to Greenville in person. I determined to see the coroner and find out what kind of a man he was. If possible, I should induce him to have Mrs. Pattmore's body exhumed and an inquest held upon it.

I had previously written to Mr. Chapman to obtain further information about the Captain and his family, and had mentioned his superstitious belief in the ring. I said that I was not afraid of losing money, as the Captain offered me more than my usual scale of prices; but the Captain's story and his great superstition led me to think that he was a "wee bit daft," and that there was insanity in the family.

Mr. Chapman replied that he had known the Captain's father and mother intimately, but there had been no sign of insanity in any of their actions. They had been, however, firm believers in their rings, and had had the rings which they had worn buried with them. They had been clear-headed, religious people, and it was surprising that they should have had such a superstitious faith in the power of those opal rings. The Captain had always been an honorable, straight-forward man, but he and his sister were even more superstitious than any of the others.

"Well," I thought, on reading Mr. Chapman's letter, "the whole family are a strange medley; but I think I can turn their superstitious credulity to good account, in my efforts to learn whether Pattmore poisoned his wife."

CHAPTER IV.

A S soon as possible, I started for Greenville, to see the
coroner; on my arrival, I was so fortunate as to
meet Mr. Wells, an old friend, who had formerly been
sheriff of the county. He offered to introduce me to his
successor, Mr. Tomlinson, who had once been his deputy.
Mr. Wells was quite wealthy, and had retired from
business. Mr. Tomlinson was an honest, hard working
carpenter, who was thoroughly reliable and zealous.
Neither of these gentlemen, however, had the shrewd-
ness nor the experience necessary to detect criminals of
the character and ability of Pattmore. They were
perfectly competent to attend to the small thieves and
swindlers of the district, but they were wholly ignorant
and unsuspicious of the means by which daring and
skillful villains carry out their plans and hide the evidences of their crimes.

They knew Mr. Pattmore well, as he had resided in
Greenville for seven years. They stated that he was a
scheming politician who could not be depended upon,
and that he was trying to get the Democratic Nomination
for congressman. Probably, he would not succeed, but
he was spending money freely. and he would, therefore,
be apt to get some good office. He was not wealthy, but
he kept his hotel well, and did a large business. Mr.
Wells thought that he used all his money as fast as he

47

made it, either in trying to get votes, or in some other way outside of his business. His wife had been generally esteemed by a large circle of acquaintances.

I told Mr. Tomlinson that I should like to see the coroner, and have him investigate the causes of Mrs. Pattmore's death.

"Oh! that will be easy," he replied, "as I know Van Valkenburgh, the coroner, very well, and we are on good terms. He is a warm friend of Pattmore,— in fact, they are boon companions. He spends most of his time in idling about the Pattmore House, and only yesterday, they went driving together."

"I am sorry to hear that," said I; "for he will not wish to do anything to injure his friend. How can I get an inquest called?"

"I don't know," said Mr. Tomlinson.

"Suppose that I should make an affidavit under an assumed name and hand it to you, could you not serve it on the coroner as a complaint which required his attention?" I asked.

"No; that would not do, as it would involve me in difficulty," replied the sheriff; "but if I should hear people talking about the death of Mrs. Pattmore, and hinting at foul play, it would be my duty to lay the matter before the coroner. Then he, as a friend of Pattmore, could not do otherwise than order an inquest."

I determined to act on this suggestion, and I therefore telegraphed to Mr. Bangs, my General Superintendent, directing him to send two of my detectives, Mr. Green and Mr. Knox, to meet me at the Clarendon House in Greenville. They left Chicago by the next train, and when they arrived in Greenville, I instructed them to go into the office of the hotel and begin a conversation about Mrs. Pattmore's death; having told them what I wished them to say, I sent them in. I had previously arranged that Mr. Tomlinson should be present. Accordingly, they took seats in the main hall in front of the clerk's desk, near which there was a large group of guests and citizens, and began to talk in loud tones.

"Well," said Knox, "there are more cases of death by poisoning than you would suppose. Now, there was a case in this town, only a short time ago, in which I think that poison was used."

"Oh! you mean Mrs. Pattmore," said Green. "Yes, that was a very suspicious affair. Was anything done about it?"

"No," replied Knox; "but every one, who knows anything about the circumstances of her death, believes that she was poisoned."

My men were soon surrounded by an excited crowd, all of whom were anxious to know the grounds upon which their suspicions were based. They replied in vague terms and insinuations, as if they knew a great deal more than they would tell. The news that Mr. Pattmore was suspected of having poisoned his wife, was soon buzzed all through the Clarendon House; and, as soon as the excitement had become general, my men slipped away and joined me in my room.

Sheriff Tomlinson was immediately appealed to by many citizens to require the coroner to investigate the matter, and he finally went to the coroner's office, accompanied by quite a crowd. When the coroner was informed of the reports in circulation, he became quite indignant.

"What! *Pattmore poison his wife!*" he exclaimed. "Why, he fairly doted on her, and, since her death, he can hardly assuage his grief. He is a gentleman in every sense of the word, and his character ought to be a sufficient protection against so gross a slander. This is a contemptible invention of his political opponents. I will soon vindicate him, however. I shall have Mrs. Pattmore's body exhumed, and shall call an inquest. Then, if any one has any charges to make, there will be an opportunity for them to come forward. I will not consent to see a friend of mine so vilely slandered."

Coroner Van Valkenburgh immediately wrote an order to have Mrs. Pattmore's body disinterred, and, also, a call for an inquest the following day. He had become very indignant at the idea of connecting his friend, Pattmore, with such a hideous crime; he, therefore, hurried over to tell Pattmore of the rumors, and of the prompt measures he had taken to prove their falsity. He drew Pattmore into a private room and told him all that he had heard and done. He expected that Pattmore would thank him heartily for his friendly action; but, instead, Pattmore's face turned very white, and he asked who it was that had spread the rumors. The coroner said that the sheriff and several prominent citizens had called upon him to investigate the rumors that were circulating at the hotels and on the street. Pattmore became very much excited when he heard this, and paced up and down in a nervous, irritable manner.

"Well," said Van Valkenburgh, "I will have the body

exhumed to-morrow, and when we have disproved the calumny, this scheme of your enemies will do you more good than harm."

"Yes," said Pattmore; "but my love for my wife is far above all other considerations. It is shocking to think that her body must be torn from the grave to refute the vile slanders of my political opponents. I do not know what course you usually pursue in such cases, but I would not, for the world, have her remains exposed to the gaze of a cruel, heartless crowd of strangers."

Mr. Pattmore's feelings quite overcame him, at the thought of such desecration, and he wept.

"I'll take care of that," said the sympathizing coroner; "I will have Dr. Forsythe make the examination, and his testimony will be sufficient for the jury."

"Well, I shall be satisfied with any arrangements you may make," said Pattmore. "I hope a good jury will be summoned; I do not wish my wife's body to be examined by a lot of curiosity seekers."

"Your wishes shall be attended to," replied the coroner. "I know who are your friends and I will summon no one else to sit on the jury."

"Van Valkenburgh," exclaimed Pattmore, seizing the coroner's hand, "I am your friend for life!"

He then led the way to the bar-room and invited the coroner to drink.

Miller was standing in the bar-room as the coroner and Pattmore passed, and noticing a haggard, pallid expression on the latter's face, he stepped up and said:

"Why, what's the matter Pattmore? Has anything gone wrong with you?"

"No, Mr. Miller, nothing very serious. Some of my enemies have started a story that I am responsible for my wife's death; but, of course, there is not a word of truth in it. The coroner has taken the matter in charge, and his verdict will soon set at rest these scandalous lies. There is nothing too sacred for these political harpies and ghouls : they literally have dragged the loved dead from the grave in the hope of injuring my reputation. Well, time will show my innocence."

So saying, Pattmore pressed Miller's hand warmly, as if overcome with emotion, and passed into the office. Mr. Green and Mr. Knox were watching him, and when he went up stairs, he was followed by Knox, who saw him go into his room. Knox immediately came down stairs and passed across the street to a corner where I had agreed to wait for him. Having heard his report I said :

" Mr. Knox, you are a stranger here, so you had better go back to see what Pattmore is doing. You can stumble into his room, as if you had mistaken it for your own. Be quick !" I added, as he started, "for we must keep watch of him every minute until the inquest has been held."

"Knox rushed into the hotel, ran up stairs and hastily entered Pattmore's room, where he found Pattmore writing a letter.

"Oh ! I beg pardon," said Knox, "I have mistaken the room," and so saying, he withdrew and returned to me.

"So he is writing a letter, is he ?" said I. "We must learn the contents of that letter, and I have not a minute to lose. Knox, find Green and Miller and bring them over here at once. Thank goodness, it is getting so dark that we shall not be noticed."

Knox was off like a shot, and in a very few minutes all my men were with me.

"Green," I said, "go to your hotel, pay your bill, and proceed to the Pattmore House. When you register your name, you must hail the clerk as an old acquaintance. This will be an easy matter, as hotel clerks are known by hundreds of people. Miller, you must be in the office at the same time, and you must both remain there until Pattmore puts his letter in the mail-box. Then, Green you must ask the clerk out to take a drink, and while you are gone, Miller must get possession of the letter. When you have secured it, come over to the Globe Hotel, where I am stopping."

Green hurried off to the Clarendon House to get his carpet-bag, and Miller returned to the Pattmore House. I also sent Knox to watch Pattmore, and to follow him wherever he might go, until he retired for the night.

Soon after Miller reached the office, Pattmore came down stairs with a letter, which Miller carefully scrutinized, so as to be able to recognize it among a group of others.

"Has the mail for the West closed yet?" asked Pattmore.

"No," replied the clerk, "there is still about an hour to spare."

Pattmore then dropped his letter into the mail-box and went out. At this moment Green stepped up to the desk, registered his name, and asked for a room. As the clerk was attending to his room and baggage, Green

"As soon as the clerk had left the office, Miller quietly extracted Pattmore's letter from the box."

looked intently at him, as if trying to recall his name. Then, stepping forward, he said, cordially :

"Why, how are you? When did you come here? Let me see; the last time I saw you was at a hotel in Buffalo, wasn't it?"

This was a lucky guess, for the clerk replied :

"Havn't you seen me since then? Why, I left there over a year ago."

"Well, I'm right glad to see you again," said Green; "step into the bar-room and take a 'smile' with me."

"I can't very well leave the office just now," said the clerk.

"Oh, yes you can," said Green; "your friend there will look after the office for a few minutes; come along."

"Wait here until I come back, will you?" the clerk asked Miller, as he went off with Green.

As soon as the clerk had left the office, Miller quietly extracted Pattmore's letter from the box. He had marked its appearance so well that he only needed one glance to identify it, and he secured it so quickly that none of the crowd outside the desk noticed any movement on his part. In a few minutes the clerk returned to the desk, and Miller lounged out into the bar-room, whence he hurried over to meet me at the Globe Hotel. He there gave me the letter, which was addressed :

"Mrs. Annie Thayer,
"Chicago,
"Illinois."

I carefully opened it by a simple process, which did not leave any evidence that the envelope had been tampered with. The letter began : "My own dear Annie," and the writer went on to caution Mrs. Thayer that she must not be alarmed at the news he was about to tell her. He said that some of his enemies had started a report that he had poisoned his late wife. He had no doubt that the Whig newspapers would spread and magnify these reports; still, he had no fears that they would be of any permanent injury to him, since his friend, coroner Van Valkenburgh, had agreed to hold an inquest, and there would be no difficulty in proving his innocence. He begged her to excuse the haste and brevity of the note, as he only had time to dash off a few lines to assure her that all was well, and to warn her not to become alarmed at anything she might see in the newspapers. The letter was signed: "Ever your loving and devoted husband,   ALONZO PATTMORE."

"Well, this is certainly strange," I meditated. "Her 'devoted *husband*,' eh? How can that be? He has had no opportunity to marry her since his wife died; hence, unless he committed bigamy, this title of 'husband' is only assumed in anticipation; yet Mrs. Thayer is, undoubtedly, beautiful and winning, and she may have induced him to ease her conscience by a form of marriage, even while his legal wife still lived. I must look into this more closely on my return to Chicago."

I then re-sealed the letter and gave it back to Mr. Miller, with instructions to return to the hotel and keep a general watch on all that went on. He was not to mail the letter until early the next morning. As Miller went out Knox came in.

"Well, Knox, what news?" I asked.

"Mr. Pattmore has gone away in a hack," replied Knox, breathlessly.

"What direction did he take?"

"He drove off at a rapid rate toward the southern part of the town, and I could not keep up, nor get on behind. I took the number of the hack, though," answered Knox.

"That was right," I remarked, as Knox paused to get his breath.

"It was number fifty-two, and the driver seemed to be an Irishman. He looked like a genial, half-grown, young fellow, and I do not think I shall have any difficulty in pumping him when he returns, as I know where his stand is."

"Right again," I exclaimed. "Now you had better wait around there until the hack returns; then get into conversation with the driver, and ask him to take a drink in the nearest saloon; while you are talking with him, you can easily learn where Pattmore went."

It was ten o'clock when Knox left me, and, as I was greatly fatigued, I went to bed immediately. Shortly after midnight, Knox again awoke me.

"What news?" I asked, starting up. "Did you succeed in learning anything from the hackman?"

"Yes," replied Knox; "he returned a little before eleven o'clock, and I asked him whether he knew where there were any young ladies I could visit. He said that he knew several places. I then asked him to take a drink while we talked about it. I said, I judged, from his appearance, that he was just the young fellow who could take me where I wanted to go; that I was crossing the street to employ him in the early part of the evening,

when he was taken by another gentleman, who probably
went to the same kind of a place that I wanted to find.
This had confirmed my opinion of the hackman, so I had
decided to await his return.   'By the way,' I added, 'was
I right about that gentleman?'   The driver laughed
loudly, and said that that was Mr. Pattmore, and that he
did not go to such places.   He went on to say that Mr.
Pattmore's wife had been dead only a few days, and he
supposed that Mr. Pattmore had gone out to pay the
grave-digger, since his visit had been made to that
individual at the graveyard gate."

"Did the boy say whether Pattmore saw the grave-
digger?" I asked.

"Yes," continued Knox; "I pumped out all that the
young fellow knew.   The grave-digger lives in a little
shanty close by the graveyard, and, on arriving there,
Pattmore called the fellow to one side, and conversed
with him in a low tone for some time.   He then paid him
some money, entered the hack, and told the boy to drive
straight back to the Pattmore House, where Pattmore
discharged the hackman.   I drew this information out of
the boy very easily, without appearing to take any special
interest in the story.   I then told him to drive me to
some quiet house where I could meet some young ladies.
He took me to a place near here, and I paid him off
immediately, saying that I should spend the night there.
As soon as he was out of sight, I came straight here,
without going into the house at all."

"By Jove!" I exclaimed, "we shall have some rough
work to-night, and we must be quick, too.   Go over to
the Pattmore House, find out from the register what room

Green is in, and wake him up as soon as possible. Tell him to come here, being careful that no one notices him, and to be sure to bring his pistols. You have yours, have you not, Mr. Knox?"

"Yes; do you expect to need them?"

"It is quite possible, as we shall have some risky work to-night. I will meet you outside, and you must tell Green to prepare for a march. Luckily we are all good walkers.

Knox hurried away, and, in a short time, both of my detectives joined me in the street. We then hired a hack and drove to within half a mile of the graveyard, where I paid off the hackman, and we entered the grounds of a residence, standing some distance back from the road. My object in entering these grounds, was to make the hackman believe we were stopping there; otherwise, his curiosity would have been excited as to my reasons for going into the country at that hour of the night. As soon as the hack was out of sight, we returned to the highway, and, after a brisk walk, we reached the grave-yard.

II

CHAPTER V.

THE resting places of the dead are localities which I do not much care to visit in the night. In the day time it is different; there is a holy calm about a cemetery then which impresses mé with a feeling of rest, and I can really enjoy an hour or two in quiet contemplation of the monuments and humble head-stones of a large burial ground. But in the night, even the least superstitious person in the world will be awed by the solemnity pervading our cities of the dead, and will quicken his pace as the wind rustles mournfully through the shrubbery. I never should care to go into a grave-yard at night, as a matter of choice; but business is business, and must be transacted, no matter how unpleasant the surroundings may be.

The first difficulty I encountered on entering the Greenville cemetery, was, that I did not know where Mrs. Pattmore's grave was located. We therefore separated to the distance of about one hundred yards, and advanced through the underbrush across the grounds. We arranged, before starting, to meet at a certain tall tree, which stood up against the sky in the dim starlight. Green had gone only a few rods when he came upon three men. Their smoky lantern threw a ghastly light upon their work, and they were so busily engaged in digging that they did not notice him. He quickly withdrew and hurried after me. It was some time after he overtook me before we could find Knox, but we finally met and returned to the place where the body-snatchers were at work. It was evident that they were professionals, for they had worked so rapidly as to have nearly succeeded in getting the coffin out of the grave.

A thrill of horror even now goes through me as I think of that night; the white tomb-stones stood forth among the foliage, by which they were surrounded, like sheeted ghosts, and the waving leaves gave them the appearance of weird shapes in fantastic motion. The light of the lantern feebly glimmered in one direction, and the body-snatchers flitted about like restless ghouls preparing for a horrible banquet. We approached as quietly as possible, and, on emerging from the cover of a copse of hazel bushes, we made a general rush forward. The ghouls were too quick for us, however, and they ran away at a break-neck speed which we did not dare to imitate. They had the great advantage of knowing every foot of the ground, while we were continually obliged to dodge around some obstruction. First, Knox stumbled headlong over a low grave, and then I became entangled in some trailing vines. As I regained my feet, I saw Green rising from an encounter with a chain which had tripped him, and we simultaneously abandoned the chase. It was clearly useless to follow them further, but we fired at them with our revolvers in the hope of frightening them into a surrender. One of them instantly stopped, returned our fire, and then continued his flight. This satisfied me that they were old hands at the business of grave-robbing, and that they were not to be scared by long-range pistol practice. After watching for a couple of hours, I returned with my men to the city, being con-vinced that the body-snatchers would not make another attempt to rob the grave. As I walked back, I tried to account, in my own mind, for this new move of Pattmore. I could not see the advantage to be gained by the removal of Mrs. Pattmore's body, and I retired to rest with that problem still unsolved.

Being greatly fatigued, it was eight o'clock next morning before I awoke. While I was at breakfast Mr. Miller came in, but he had nothing to report, except that Patt-more seemed greatly troubled, and looked very haggard. I ordered Miller to watch Pattmore closely, and to engage him in conversation as much as possible. I then went in search of Sheriff Tomlinson, whom I soon found. Believ-ing him to be a thoroughly trustworthy man, I related to him all that had occurred the night before. He was much astonished at my story, and said that he was sorry I had not asked him to accompany me, as he knew the graveyard well. If the body-snatchers had been caught, they might have been able to give very important testi-mony at the inquest. Pattmore might have been held to appear before the grand jury on their testimony alone.

"Yes," I replied; "no one regrets their escape more than I do; but I am almost equally annoyed by the fact that I cannot reach a satisfactory conclusion as to Pattmore's motive in having his wife's body carried off. Of course, if the coroner's men should have found the body gone, every one would suspect Pattmore of having had it removed. However, I propose to solve the mystery in some way. By the way, Mr. Tomlinson, when do you expect the body to arrive?"

"It will be here by eleven o'clock, and the men having it in charge, will take it directly to Coroner Van Valkenburgh's office."

"I suppose he will impanel a jury," I remarked.

"Certainly," the sheriff replied; "and it would be well for you to be present to watch the proceedings. Pattmore must be made to face the music in some way."

Accordingly, I watched the coroner's office until I saw the hearse arrive, and, when the coffin was carried in, I followed it. The coroner's assistants reported that some body-snatchers had been at work, and had attempted to steal Mrs. Pattmore's body, having succeeded in getting the coffin nearly out of the grave; but they had evidently been interrupted, as they had left all their tools behind, and had not tried to open the coffin. They had been more successful in another case, however; the body of a woman had been taken from a grave in the Potter's Field, (which was devoted to paupers, etc.) and had been carried to a spot near Mrs. Pattmore's grave. The supposition was that the robbers, wishing to procure female subjects for dissection, had chosen those two graves as containing the bodies of persons who had most recently died.

On hearing this story, I saw through the trick at a glance. The sheriff was in the office, and I beckoned to him to join me outside.

"Mr. Tomlinson," I said, "I wish you to send a man to the graveyard to learn the name of the other woman, whose body was found; get a description of her age, height, size, and general appearance, as I feel sure that

Pattmore's intention was, to substitute her body for that of his wife."

"By Jupiter! that's so!" exclaimed Mr. Tomlinson; "but I should never have thought of that. I will attend to your request myself, while you can remain here to watch the proceedings before the coroner. I will go to the cemetery and make a thorough investigation. It is my duty to become acquainted with all the facts in the case," and he started off, accompanied by Mr. Green, whom I sent with him.

In a short time, Pattmore walked into the office and sat down. He wore a martyr-like expression, and, though he controlled his feelings sufficiently to appear outwardly calm, I could see that, inwardly, he was racked with fear and nervousness.

The coroner hastily impaneled a jury, consisting wholly of Pattmore's personal and political friends. The coffin was then opened, as a matter of form, and the jury merely looked at the rapidly decaying corpse. Pattmore refused to look at the body, on the ground that he did not wish to mar the sweet memories of his beloved wife's features, which he had seen only in the flush of life and beauty, even by a glance at her merely mortal remains in their present condition.

Dr. Forsythe testified that he had attended the late Mrs. Pattmore in her last illness, and that dysentery was the cause of her death. He was corroborated by another physician who had been in consultation with Dr. Forsythe during the last day or two of the patient's life. As no other witnesses were called, the jury immediately returned a verdict that Mrs. Pattmore's death had resulted from natural causes; namely, dysentery.

I was watching Pattmore closely during the interval before the verdict was delivered, and I saw plainly that, in spite of the farcical character of the inquest, he was in a state of nervous dread lest something unforeseen should occur to reveal his criminality. When the verdict was read, an expression of relief and triumph came into his face, and he received the congratulations of his friends like a man who had just escaped a great danger. I had too little evidence to warrant me in showing my hand at that time, by accusing him in person; nevertheless, I was satisfied of his guilt, and I decided to use other means to bring him to justice.

In about an hour, Sheriff Tomlinson returned from the graveyard, with Mr. Wells and Mr. Green. They had made notes of the condition in which they had found Mrs. Pattmore's grave, and they had written out a full description of the other corpse found near by. The body was that of a woman of about the same size, age, and general appearance as Mrs. Pattmore.

I had heard of an eminent physician in Greenville, named Dr. Stuart. On inquiring for him, Mr. Tomlinson took me to the doctor's office and introduced me. He was a man of great ability, and he had a high reputation throughout the West as a scientific analytical chemist.

I at once laid the facts in the Pattmore case before him, and said that I wished him to analyze carefully the contents of the stomach and bowels of the late Mrs. Pattmore, in order to determine whether she had been poisoned. I said that it was a difficult case to undertake, owing to Pattmore's political influence; but I felt sure that a thorough investigation would establish his guilt beyond question.

The Doctor replied that, under most circumstances, he should hardly feel inclined to comply with such a request, since he had no right to make such an analysis, unless he had the consent of the relatives of the deceased; or, upon the coroner's order. Still, he had a natural desire for fair play, and the facts which I had presented to him seemed to point toward the possibility that a foul crime had been committed; hence, he would perform the analysis, provided that his action should never be made known to any one, until he should be called upon to testify in court. Of course, if no trace of poison should be found, the theory of death by that means would have to be abandoned, and his connection with the affair need never be disclosed.

"I have never met you before, Mr. Pinkerton," concluded Dr. Stuart, "but your reputation is well known to me, and I feel sure that you would not have made this request unless there were strong reasons for such action. I have full confidence in you, and I will give you all the aid in my power. Where is Mrs. Pattmore's body now?"

"It is in the coroner's office," I replied, "and it will be taken back to the grave in about an hour."

"Well, Mr. Pinkerton, can't you obtain possession of it in some way? I shall only want it for a short time."

"That is what puzzles me," I replied; "I am afraid Pattmore will follow the body to the grave."

"Then, if he should do so, can't you get two men who

know how to handle a shovel quickly, to disinter it a second time?" asked the Doctor.

"Yes; I will take two of my own men," I said; "I can trust them more than any one else."

"Oh, nonsense!" exclaimed the Doctor, laughing, "you can do better than that. You had better offer the regular grave-diggers ten dollars to leave the body a short time in your possession before burying it; or, if Pattmore should insist upon seeing it buried, they can easily disinter it for you, and it will take me only a short time to remove the intestines. I shall then seal them up for the present, as I am too busy to make the analysis just now; but when I shall have finished my present work, I will take up this case. You can depend upon hearing from me at the earliest possible moment."

It was then arranged that Mr. Wells and sheriff Tomlinson should be present to witness the removal of the bowels from Mrs. Pattmore's body; the sheriff further decided to give an official order for the analysis, so as to protect Dr. Stuart in case of any accident. If any signs of poison were found, the Doctor's charges would be paid by the county; otherwise I should be responsible for the amount. I then went out to see the grave-diggers, and used such convincing arguments that they willingly agreed to disinter the body. My arguments were brief, but cogent, and were presented to them about in the following way:

"Mr. Grave-digger, you look like a man of discretion, who knows how to open his hands and shut his mouth. I wish to obtain the body of the late Mrs. Pattmore for a short time. I will give you several excellent reasons why

you will be willing to let me have it. In the first
place, I will give you twenty-five dollars for the job;
secondly, ——"

"Wa-al, I guess you needn't go any furder," drawled
the grave-digger, with a knowing wink; "twenty-five
o' them reasons are enough for me; so just tell me
where you want the body, and I'll see that it's forth-
coming."

I have always found that half the argument may be
dispensed with if the matter is only *presented in the proper
light.*

In accordance with the agreement, therefore, the body
was again taken from the grave in the presence of Mr.
Wells, Sheriff Tomlinson, Dr. Stuart, my detectives, and
myself; the necessary parts were removed by the Doctor,
and the body was re-buried; finally, the Doctor placed
the portions which had been removed in a jar of alcohol,
and it was then sealed up to await the Doctor's analysis.

Of one thing I felt certain; and that was, that the
regular grave-diggers and the body-snatchers of the night
before were the same persons; hence, I feared that they
might give Pattmore information of our proceedings. I
communicated my opinion to the Sheriff, and suggested
that a slight hint from him might induce the men to keep
silence for their own protection. Accordingly he spoke
to them about the occurrence of the previous night, and
said that for the present he did not intend to make any
investigation to learn who were the body-snatchers on
that occasion.

"But," he added, significantly, "if I ever discover that
Mr. Pattmore, or any one else, has been informed of this

action which I have just taken, I shall consider it my duty as Sheriff, to bring to punishment immediately the men who attempted to rob this grave last night—*and I don't think I shall have any trouble in finding them.*"

While returning to the city, I impressed upon Sheriff Tomlinson the necessity of procuring all the evidence that could be reached relative to Mrs. Pattmore's death. I asked him particularly to find the nurses who attended her, and to learn all that they could tell about the symptoms of the patient; the kind and amount of medicines administered; the effect of the doses; and, in general, all the particulars of Mrs. Pattmore's illness and death. The Sheriff promised to do all in his power, and Mr. Wells also agreed to give his assistance in bringing out the whole truth.

On arriving at the Globe Hotel I met Miller, who gave me a copy of a letter which Pattmore had written to Mrs. Thayer, as soon as the coroner's jury had given their verdict. The letter contained a brief account of the inquest and the finding of the jury. It said that she could understand his feelings of great relief that all had turned out so well for him. The letter was signed, as in the former case, "Your loving husband."

Mr. Miller said that Pattmore's manner had wholly changed since the close of the inquest; before he had been morose and irritable; now he was all vivacity and good spirits. One of his first acts, after the verdict had been given, was to write the above-mentioned letter, which Miller had secured as before. Having taken a copy of it, Miller had mailed it in the general post-office.

"You have done very well, Mr. Miller," I said, "and I

wish you to remain here to watch Pattmore's movements and intercept his letters. I shall return to Chicago tonight, and you must inform me by telegraph if Pattmore leaves here."

Having completed all my arrangements, I returned to Chicago, taking Knox and Green with me.

CHAPTER VI.

M Y first action, on reaching my office, was to send for Mrs. Kate Warne, the Superintendent of the Female Department of my force. She made a full report of all the work in her charge during my absence, and brought up among other cases, that of Captain Sumner.

"Miss Seaton," said Mrs. Warne, "reports that she has progressed somewhat toward an intimacy with Mrs. Thayer, but that she has learned very little except by observation. Mrs. Thayer seems to be greatly troubled at times, but she is very reserved, and does not appear anxious to make any one her confidant. She goes to the post-office regularly twice a day, but she rarely goes anywhere else. Once she went to a druggist's store, but, being unable to get what she wanted, she entered another one and purchased a small package."

"Has Miss Seaton been able to examine any of Mrs. Thayer's trunks or bureau drawers?" I asked.

"Only once," replied Mrs. Warne; "she succeeded in getting into one of her trunks, and there found an immense quantity of letters signed 'Alonzo Pattmore,' some of them dating back several years."

"Were they long, sentimental and — in short, were they to be classed under the head of love letters?" I asked, with a smile.

"Yes; Miss Seaton so reports them."

"Well," I said, "let her continue to watch Mrs. Thayer, and to seek to win the latter's confidence. By the way, what kind of books does Mrs. Thayer read?"

"Oh! anything that is romantic."

"Then, tell Miss Seaton to get 'Eugene Aram' and read it. She can make such allusions to it as will make Mrs. Thayer wish to read it too. The effect of the story on her mind will, perhaps, prepare her for the train of thoughts which I wish to excite in her."

"Oh! that reminds me," said Mrs. Warne, "Mrs. Thayer complains that she sleeps very poorly, and dreams a great deal. She has been wondering whether she talks in her sleep."

At this moment, one of my clerks entered and said that Captain Sumner wished to see me. I immediately sent word that he could come into my private office; at the same time, I requested Mrs. Warne to step into the next room for a few minutes, as I should need her, as soon as the Captain had gone. When the Captain entered, I was busily engaged in examining some papers, and I greeted him as if he were an old friend whom I had not seen for months.

"Why, how are you, Captain Sumner?" I said, shaking his hand, warmly. "I am delighted to see you."

"I'm pretty well," he replied; "but have you heard the news?"

"No; what news?"

"Read that," he said, handing me the Greenville *Advocate*, and pointing to an account of the inquest on Mrs. Pattmore's body.

The paper contained a full report of the coroner's proceedings, and an editorial on the subject. The editor
spoke in the highest terms of Pattmore, and congratulated
him on his triumphant vindication. I read all that the
Advocate contained relative to the case, and then remarked:

"I wonder who started that investigation."

"I can't imagine," replied the Captain; "though, as
the paper says, the story might have been originated by
his enemies, for mere political effect."

"Yes; that is possible," I replied; "but there was no
use in attempting anything of that kind. The result
must have strengthened him, even among his opponents."

"I am afraid so, too," said the Captain. "We shall
have a hard time in obtaining any proofs of his guilt, now
that he is so popular."

I saw that the Captain did not suspect that I had been
connected, in any way, with the Greenville inquest; I
therefore, changed the subject.

"Well, it will all come out right, if you have patience.
How is Mrs. Thayer?"

"Not at all well," he replied; "she is very restless, and
she complains of being nervous; besides, she is more
reserved with me than ever. Don't you think I had
better try to induce her to go home with me? I should
feel more comfortable if she were on the farm in Connecticut, as she would then be out of Pattmore's power.
Sometimes I think there is no use in trying to reform her;
for, she seems so infatuated with that man that I only
wonder she has not run away with him before now. I
know that she will marry him at the first opportunity."

"We must prevent that," I replied; "for the present, I think she had better remain here."

I then asked the Captain to excuse me a moment, and, stepping into the next room, I called my stenographer to the door; by leaving the door ajar, the conversation between the Captain and myself could be easily heard in the next room. The short-hand writer, therefore, was able to take down everything that was said. Returning to the Captain, I commenced a friendly chat, in the course of which, I led him on to talk about his family. I especially desired to draw out the particulars of Annie's history, and the honest old gentleman talked so freely that I obtained a very full account of all that he knew about her. In the conversation which we had about his own affairs, the Captain gave me the following story to account for the fact that he was an old bachelor:

"It seems somewhat strange," he said, "that I am unmarried, as I have always been a great admirer of the fair sex; but, the fact is, I had one strong affection, and that has lasted me all my life. The last time I was with her, she promised to be my wife, and we pledged ourselves to be eternally faithful to each other. I sailed for Singapore the next day, and, on my return, I was to lead her to the altar. I felt that I had secured a prize far beyond my merits, for she seemed to be superior to me in every way. The days dragged along slowly and wearily, while on the voyage; but, at length, we returned to New York. I immediately hurried up from the landing-place, all impatient to see my sweetheart. As I passed up the dock, I met an old acquaintance.

" 'Where away so fast?' he asked, as he stopped me.

" 'I am going to see Miss Curtis,' I replied.

" ' Why, she married a rich banker, six months ago,' he said.

" 'Oh! did she?' I exclaimed; 'I am glad she was so fortunate.'

" Then I returned aboard ship, feeling completely crushed. Since that time I have never paid attention to any other woman, for I can never forget her. Once afterward I met her on Broadway, on her way to her carriage. She nodded carelessly, with a ' How d'ye do, John?' and was quickly whirled away out of my sight. I have never heard from her since then.

After the Captain had told me everything about Annie and himself that he could recollect, I asked him to excuse me, pleading an important engagement at that hour. As soon as he had gone, I requested my steno-grapher to write out his notes in long hand as quickly as possible, and I returned to consult with my female superintendent.

"Mrs. Warne," I said, "we shall have a difficult task in working upon Mrs. Thayer; she seems to be very reticent and wary. I have decided to attack the super-stitious side of her nature, which seems to be her weakest point; and, in order to do so successfully, I shall need your services. How do you think you would succeed as a fortune-teller?"

"A fortune-teller!" she exclaimed, laughingly; "that is certainly a new *role ;* however, I think I might learn to take the part after a few lessons."

"Yes," I replied, "the tricks of the trade are easily
12

learned. Here is a book which explains all the secrets
of the profession. It is called 'The Mysteries of Magic
and the Wonders of Astrology; by Dr. Roback.' You
can take it to read at your leisure; but, after all, the costume and make-up are the principal things necessary.
You will be obliged to trust largely to your own judgment and tact in working upon Mrs. Thayer's feelings.
I suppose she has some vague ideas about astrology, etc.,
but I have no doubt of your ability to mystify her
thoroughly. One thing is certain, Mrs. Warne, that we
must have a fortune-teller of our own, and I do not know
of any one so competent as yourself. I will rent an office
for you near by, and the duties will interfere very little
with your other work."

"I will undertake it," she said, decidedly, after a
moment's thought; "I will make it a success, too, if you
will give me my own way about it."

"All right," I answered; "success is all that I require."

Mrs. Warne then withdrew to make her preparations.

In a day or two I received a letter from Miller. He
said that the talk over the inquest was gradually sub-
siding; that there were some few persons who were not
fully satisfied with the manner of conducting the inquiry,
but that the general effect had been favorable to Pattmore; that the latter had began to drink a great deal,
though not enough to become intoxicated; that he,
(Miller,) had been taken into Pattmore's confidence to a
considerable extent; and that the latter had expressed an
intention of going to Cincinnati to make a visit. In
conclusion, he said that Pattmore was doing his utmost

to appear cheerful, but that he looked very haggard, and seemed to be in great trouble.

Miss Seaton reported to Mrs. Warne the same day, that she was becoming more intimate with Mrs. Thayer, though the latter manifested no desire to take any one into her confidence. The day previous Mrs. Thayer had gone to the post-office, where she had received a letter, as usual. She had torn it open, as if very anxious to learn the news it contained for her, and had then crumpled it nervously in her hand, after reading it.

Miss Seaton also described a scene which had taken place that morning. Mrs. Thayer was in her room about eleven o'clock; soon afterward Miss Seaton went to the door and knocked. No answer being given, she went in quietly, intending to surprise Mrs. Thayer. She found the latter deeply absorbed in telling her own fortune with a pack of cards. Miss Seaton laughed pleasantly, and said:

"So you were telling your fortune, were you? Well, how did it come out?"

Mrs. Thayer looked somewhat confused at first, but she gathered up the cards mechanically, and said:

"I don't know how to tell my fortune; do you?"

"Yes, indeed, I used to be a splendid fortune-teller," replied Miss Seaton. "Let me try to tell your fortune."

She then shuffled the cards, dealt them in three piles, and turned up the last card, which happened to be the queen of hearts.

"Now let us see what your fortune *has* been, what it *is*, and what it *will* be," said Miss Seaton. "You are represented by the queen of hearts; this pile contains your past; that one your present; and the third your future."

So saying, she turned up the top card of each pile. By an odd coincidence the present and future were both clubs, the past being a diamond.

Miss Seaton said, gravely:

"Your past has been pleasant, but your future is unpromising."

"Yes, it is always so," replied Mrs. Thayer, despondently.

Then, as Miss Seaton was about to go on, Mrs. Thayer threw all the cards into a heap, saying:

"No, I don't want to hear any more; I shall have the same luck throughout; clubs always come to me."

"Have you always had such bad fortune?" asked Miss Seaton.

"Oh! no; only a few years ago, I used to be as happy as a bird; sorrow was unknown to me, and one enjoyment seemed to pass away only to be succeeded by another. Now I have nothing but trouble all the time."

"Your lot seems hard," remarked Miss Seaton, in a sympathizing tone; "probably you feel worse since your husband has been dead."

"Dead!" exclaimed Mrs. Thayer, springing up; then, recovering her presence of mind, she sat down, muttering: "yes, yes, of course, he's dead."

"What do you mean?" said Miss Seaton. "Is it long since he died?"

"I do not feel well to-day; and I shall not try to read my fortune again when I am so nervous," replied Mrs. Thayer, evading Miss Seaton's question.

Seeing that Mrs. Thayer wished to change the subject, Miss Seaton did not press her further. The two ladies remained together until dinner time, and Miss Seaton read a portion of " Eugene Aram " aloud. Mrs. Thayer became deeply interested in the book, and borrowed it to read.

Next morning I received a telegram from Miller, briefly stating that Pattmore had left Greenville. His destination was Chicago, though he had given out that he was going to Cincinnati.

I knew that he could not arrive that day, as the railroad connections were not promptly made at that time; but I instructed Mr. Knox and Mr. Green to be prepared to "shadow" him, on his arrival at the depot the next morning, and to keep upon his track constantly, while he remained in Chicago. I also sent word to Miss Seaton to make some pretense for calling upon Mrs. Thayer early in the forenoon, and to remain with her as long as possible. I knew that Pattmore would communicate with Mrs. Thayer immediately on his arrival, and my object was, to have some one to witness their meeting.

On entering my office early the next day, I was surprised to find Captain Sumner awaiting me, in a great state of excitement.

"That man has come here again, Mr. Pinkerton," he broke out, impetuously. " He came before breakfast and went straight to Annie's room. I called her to the door and expostulated with her, until she agreed to send him away as soon as possible. I then came here directly to inform you."

"Quite right, Captain," I replied; "there is nothing

like taking prompt action in such cases.   You can return to the house now, and trust to me for the rest."

"But I'm afraid she will run away with that villain," said the Captain.

"Of course, we must prevent that," I replied; "I shall have a plan prepared, in case they attempt to run away together; but, I do not think Pattmore is quite ready yet for such a step.   Keep your spirits up, Captain, and don't borrow trouble."

"I have all confidence in you, Mr. Pinkerton," he said as he went out; "but I shall be much happier when I am back on my farm."

According to instructions, Miss Seaton called on Mrs. Thayer, though she did not gain admittance to her room. When Mrs. Thayer opened the door, Miss Seaton saw that she had been crying, and that she was evidently much disturbed.   She asked Miss Seaton to excuse her, as she had company from the East.

About noon Pattmore returned to his hotel, as the Captain would not permit him to dine at the boarding house.   As Mrs. Thayer did not come down to dinner, Miss Seaton again visited her, and found her dressing to go out.   She asked Miss Seaton to remain until she was dressed, but said that she was going out driving in the afternoon and to the theatre in the evening.   In a short time, the Captain came in, and Miss Seaton retired.   The Captain asked Mrs. Thayer what she meant by breaking her promises not to see Pattmore again.

She replied that Pattmore was a man she could not help loving; that she had tried her best to overcome her passion, but in vain; and that she could not break off the connection so abruptly, but that she would endeavor to do so gradually in the future. Then she kissed the Captain, saying that she was never so happy in her life, and that she was going out driving with Pattmore that afternoon. The Captain remonstrated with her without effect; and, seeing that he could not move her from her purpose, he came straight to my office to report.

Pattmore came again in the afternoon and took Mrs. Thayer out driving. She looked superb as she went off, having recovered entirely from her illness. She was in a perfect flutter of happiness and excitement, which gave her a brilliant color, and added to the brightness of her eyes. She was agitated by conflicting influences; on one side, was her brother, determined to separate her from her lover, and justly blaming her course; on the other, was Pattmore, claiming her love, and urging her to abandon her brother's protection.

They were gone about three hours, and, on their return, they seemed very complacent and much less excited than when they set out. In the evening, they went to the theatre together, being "shadowed" by Mr. Knox. He took a seat close behind them, in order to listen to their conversation; but he overheard nothing of any consequence.

Captain Sumner had a long talk with his sister next morning, in relation to their return to Connecticut. He begged her to go immediately, and thus escape from Pattmore's influence; but she opposed his wish, on the ground that she was too weak to make the journey. He then lost his temper, and replied that she was strong enough to go around to places of amusement with

Pattmore, and it was very strange that she could not travel slowly home. This show of anger on the Captain's part, caused her to commence crying, as she knew that he could not resist so powerful an appeal to his sympathy. The result equalled her anticipations. The Captain soon lost all his irritation and began to console her, as if she were a spoilt child; finally, she induced him to go driving with them that afternoon. The Captain told me afterward, that Pattmore behaved with great propriety during the drive, and that they did not seem to be so much in love with each other as he had supposed. I smiled inwardly at the old sailor's simplicity; for I noticed that they had gone out in an open barouche, (instead of a close carriage, such as they had used the day before,) and they had remained away only one hour, instead of three.

On their return from the drive, Pattmore and Annie went to Mrs. Thayer's sitting room, and the Captain went down town. At four o'clock, Miss Seaton knocked at Mrs. Thayer's door; but, receiving no answer, she tried to enter quietly. She found that the door was locked on the inside, however, and she was, therefore, obliged to withdraw to her own room to watch. It was six o'clock before Pattmore came out, having been nearly three hours in Mrs. Thayer's room with the door locked.

Mr. Knox "shadowed" Pattmore on his departure from the boarding house, and saw him take the nine o'clock train for Greenville. I immediately notified Mr. Miller by telegraph, directing him to renew his intimacy with Pattmore, and to remain in Greenville until further orders.

CHAPTER VII.

MR. MILLER was not idle during the time that Pattmore was away. His first action was to learn who were the nurses attending Mrs. Pattmore in her last illness. One of them had left the city, but the other, being an old resident of Greenville, was soon found. She was quite an elderly woman, with no family except one daughter. The latter was a seamstress, and Mr. Miller soon made her acquaintance by employing her to make some shirts for him. He kept up friendly relations with them by taking both mother and daughter out riding occasionally in the summer evenings; and in various ways he ingratiated himself into the old lady's confidence. It was not long before he was able to draw out all the particulars of Mrs. Pattmore's illness.

He learned that when she first became seriously sick, Mr. Pattmore began to show a very tender solicitude for her health.

He even insisted upon preparing her medicine and giving it to her himself. Mrs. Pattmore, however, did not seem to appreciate his watchful care, for she told the nurse that she did not like to take her medicine from her husband; she also asked very particularly whether the medicine which she took was that which the doctor prescribed.

Mrs. Reed, the nurse, said that she did not like the effects of the medicine at all. It was put up in small yellow papers, and when Mrs. Pattmore took a dose of it she was always taken with violent vomiting; her bowels and stomach would become very hot, and the pain would be so severe as to cause her to scream terribly. Then Mr. Pattmore would give her a dose of another kind of medicine, which would soon relieve the patient and cause her to fall into a deep sleep.

When Dr. Forsythe called, Mrs. Pattmore always informed him very carefully about the effect of the medicine, but he treated it as a case of common occurrence, and said that those symptoms invariably accompanied an attack of dysentery. After the Doctor had gone, Mr. Pattmore would return to the room with the same medicine, and his wife would exclaim:

"Oh! has the Doctor ordered that horrid medicine again? I cannot stand it long. Oh! what shall I do?"

Then her husband would tell her that it pained him almost as much as herself to see her suffer so, and that he would willingly take it himself if he could thereby save her from pain; but she must recollect that she was very dangerously sick, and that a failure to obey the Doctor's instructions might prove fatal to her. Mrs. Pattmore would be too feeble to protest long, and she would take the medicine; the same symptoms as before would then result, and each day she seemed to grow weaker and weaker.

The day of Mrs. Pattmore's death the Doctor was unable to call; hence only Mr. Pattmore and Mrs. Reed were present when she died. Pattmore spoke very endearingly to his wife and tried to caress her, but she pushed him away, gave him one long, reproachful look, and fell back dead. Pattmore professed to be overcome with grief, and tears flowed down his cheeks, as he requested Mrs. Reed to arrange for the funeral, and to spare no expense. He stopped at the door as he was leaving the room and said :

" By the way, Mrs. Reed, if any one inquires about it, you can say that dysentery was the cause of my beloved wife's death."

Miller said that there was little doubt that Mrs. Reed suspected foul play in connection with Mrs. Pattmore's death ; but she was a very discreet woman, and would not spread any story which she could not prove. It was only by very skillful management that he had been able to induce her to talk upon the subject at all. She knew that Pattmore was very popular, and that she would be speedily silenced if she attempted to suggest anything against his character ; hence she preferred to keep her suspicions to herself.

On receiving this report from Miller, I sent him instructions to continue his acquaintance with Mrs. Reed, and to keep a close watch upon her movements, for it was possible that she, too, might be induced to go away. As she would be an important witness, it would be necessary not to lose sight of her. At the end of the week I received another report from Miller, stating that Pattmore had called a select meeting of his political supporters in the district, and had laid the plans for an energetic effort to obtain the Congressional nomination. Miller had been taken into their confidence, and he was working hard to secure the election of Pattmore delegates to the approaching convention. This gave him ample opportunity to become intimate with Pattmore, and he felt sure that the latter would not take any important steps without consulting him.

I was much pleased to hear this news, as it showed me that Pattmore was no longer in fear of detection; moreover, it satisfied me that politics would detain him in Greenville for some time, and there would be no immediate danger of his marriage with Mrs. Thayer. Having a prospect that he would not return to Chicago to interfere with my plan for some weeks, I decided to proceed with my attack on Mrs. Thayer's credulity and superstition. In the afternoon, therefore, I sent for Mrs. Warne, and asked whether she had secured rooms in which to play the part of a fortune-teller.

"Yes," she replied, "I have rented three rooms on Clark street, which are just suited for the purpose. There are two entrances, so that you can slip in at any time without being seen by my visitors."

"Well, you had better have them fitted up as soon as possible. I will drop in to look at them to-day."

"No," she answered, "I don't wish you to come until I have completed my preparations. The rooms are on the second floor, and have not been occupied for some time; hence they will need considerable cleaning. You are too busy to attend to the furnishing and arranging, so I will relieve you of all the trouble; only give me *carte-blanche* for the purpose of furnishing the rooms, and I know you will not regret it."

"All right," said I; "you have my permission to do as you please, and you can get whatever money you need from the cashier. All I ask is that everything be done in the best manner. When you are ready to begin operations let me know, so that I can have an audience with the great fortune-teller in advance of the general public."

During the next four days, nothing of any consequence occurred. The Captain reported that his sister was gaining so fast in health and strength that he thought she was able to go back to Connecticut. Of course, I was obliged to oppose the journey at that time, since I wished to bring Mrs. Thayer before my fortune-teller. Miss Seaton reported that she was on quite intimate terms with Mrs. Thayer; but the latter never talked about her own affairs. She wrote daily to Pattmore, and received daily letters in reply.

At length, Mrs. Warne reported that her temple of magic was in complete order, and that she would be ready to receive me that afternoon.

"Very well," I replied; "I will drop in to have my fortune told about three o'clock. Have you arranged it wholly to your own satisfaction?"

"Yes; it is nearly perfect."

"Whom have you engaged for an usher?" I inquired.

"You must not ask questions now," she answered, laughing. "I have taken more liberties than I ever dared to take before; but I think, when you consider the object to be gained, that you will be satisfied."

"Well, I hope your rooms are as mysterious as your answers would lead me to expect," said I. "However, I shall be there promptly at three o'clock, so I will restrain my curiosity for the present."

At the appointed hour, therefore, I called at the rooms,

where I was received by a young negro of the blackest type. He was dressed in full Turkish costume, and his actions gave me the impression that he was dumb. This black mute first ushered me into a very large front room, elegantly furnished in the style of a modern *salon.* Heavy curtains hung in graceful folds from richly gilded cornices, sufficiently obscuring the windows to prevent the strong glare of the afternoon sun from penetrating directly into the room; arm-chairs and sofas were plentifully scattered about, to accommodate the throng of persons who were expected to visit the fortune-teller; the walls were hung with engravings and paintings; and on the floor was a thick Brussels carpet. into which my feet sank noiselessly, as I walked about inspecting the pictures and furniture. After scanning the sable usher for a few minutes, I said:

"Now, if that color would wash off, I should feel sure of finding one of my office boys, named Jack Scott, underneath." The mute grinned responsively, and I saw that I had guessed correctly. "Well, Jack," I continued, "I don't think you need fear detection. Where is Mrs. Warne?"

Jack still remained mute; but he went into another room, and soon beckoned me to follow him. As I crossed the threshold, the door closed noiselessly behind me. It took me several seconds to accustom my eyes to the change in the light. Then I began to gather an idea of the surroundings, and my surprise at Mrs. Warne's success was equalled only by my admiration of her good taste and judgment.

The room was nearly square, but a large mirror, at the end opposite the entrance, gave a duplicate view of the whole; the shape of the mirror being that of a large doorway, the effect was to give an appearance of two rooms, instead of one. The walls and windows were hung with some dark colored material, which wholly shut out every ray of sunlight; but a soft, dim radiance was shed from five swinging lamps, one in each corner and the fifth in the centre of the room. These lamps were of bronzed silver, of Oriental patterns, and were all in motion; the corner lamps swinging back and forth toward the centre, and the centre one, swinging slowly around in a circle. On the walls, were hung several charts and mystic symbols, while the floor was covered with a close matting of white straw, upon which was painted the common representation of the signs of the zodiac. A number of small globes stood upon a low shelf in one corner, and on a table in the centre of the room was a large globe standing on a chart. With the exception of one large easy-chair and a lounge, there were no other articles of furniture in the room. A pair of skeletons stood facing each other, one at each side of the mirror, and their ghastly appearance, duplicated in the mirror, added to the unnatural effect. Near the table was a small portable furnace upon which stood a peculiarly shaped retort, and from this, issued a pungent, aromatic incense.

While I was examining the globe and chart, Mrs. Warne slipped into the room, through the folds of a curtain at one side of the mirror, and swept down toward me. I should hardly have known her, so great was her disguise; her face and hands were stained a clear olive, and her hair hung down in heavy masses to her waist; her dress was of rich material, trimmed with Oriental extravagance; the sleeves were large and flowing, and the skirt trailed over a yard. In her right hand she carried a small wand, around which two serpents twined. Her whole appearance was dignified and imposing. The light and atmosphere added to the general effect, and I felt wholly satisfied with Mrs. Warne's work.

"Well, Mrs. Warne," said I, "you have certainly made a great success; but I am afraid I shall not be so much pleased when the bills come in."

"Don't be very much alarmed on that score," replied Mrs. Warne. "I have been very economical. Many of the most expensive articles have been hired for the occasion, while the rest have been picked up cheap at auction sales. The expense, I assure you, will not be great."

"All right," I rejoined; "the Captain will have to foot the bill, whatever it may be; but, if we succeed in our object, he will not have any reason to regret the cost."

Mrs. Warne showed me the door through which she had entered, and asked me to seat myself behind the curtains. She then called her usher into the room, and conversed with him; though they spoke in low tones, I was able to hear every word. The door where I was sitting, was hung on noiseless hinges, and it led into the last room of the suite; from this room, another door opened on a hall leading to a pair of side stairs. I was thus able to reach my ambush without entering by the front way.

"Now, Mrs. Warne, nothing remains to be done but to advertise you thoroughly," I said, after I had inspected all her preparations.

"Very well," she replied; "but you must recollect that

I shall not be able to oversee all my general work, unless you make my office hours as a fortune-teller very short. Three hours will be the longest time I can spare daily."

I then returned to my office and wrote out the following advertisement:

THE GREAT ASIATIC SIBYL,

L. L. LUCILLE, the only living descendant of Hermes,
the Egyptian, who has traveled through all the
known parts of the world, now makes her first
appearance in Chicago. She will cast
the horoscope of all callers; will
tell them the events of their
past life, and reveal what
the future has in store
for them. She has
cast the horo-
scope of
all the
c r o w n e d
heads of Eu-
rope, Asia, Africa,
and Oceanica; she will
cast the horoscope, or celes-
tial map, for the hour and moment of the inquiry for any visitor
with the same care, and by the same
method as that used in the case of the Sultan
of Turkey, and the Pacha of Trincomalee. She
will remain only a short time in Chicago; hence the
SORROWFUL AND AFFLICTED,
who wish to know what the future has in store for them,

13

had better CALL AT ONCE.

She will tell

WHO LOVES YOU; WHO HATES YOU;

and who is trying to injure you.

She will show you

YOUR FUTURE HUSBAND OR WIFE.

L. L. LUCILLE is the

Seventh Daughter of

a Seventh Daughter.

She never fails to give satisfaction.

Visit her and learn your fate.

Office hours—10 a. m. to 1 p. m.

Fee $10.00.

OFFICE AT THE TEMPLE OF MAGIC,

50 SOUTH CLARK STREET.

This advertisement was inserted in the daily newspapers for a week, and I also had a number of small handbills printed for distribution in the street. In this way Lucille's name was brought before the public very conspicuously. At that time the trade of fortune-telling was not so common as it is now, and those engaged in it rarely had the means to advertise themselves so extensively; hence Lucille's half column in the newspapers attracted an unusual amount of attention.

CHAPTER VIII.

THE next morning Miss Seaton called on Mrs. Thayer as usual, and found her eagerly reading Lucille's advertisement in one of the newspapers. Miss Seaton asked Mrs. Thayer whether she was ready to go out for their regular morning walk, and Mrs. Thayer soon prepared to accompany her. They first went to the post-office; and, as they walked away, after Mrs. Thayer had received a letter, they met a boy distributing hand-bills. They each took one and walked along slowly in order to read Lucille's glowing advertisement. Mrs. Thayer folded her bill up carefully and said :

"I wonder whether this woman can do what she claims; if I thought so, I would call on her myself."

"Well, I don't have much faith in these people, as a rule," replied Miss Seaton, "but it is a fact that some of them really have a strange and inexplicable power to foresee events. Whether it is a genuine science, or a mere application of general rules of physiognomy to the particular features of each visitor, I do not profess to say; but there is no doubt, I believe, that they have been very successful in reading the future for some people."

"I am so glad to hear you say that," said Mrs. Thayer, "for I was afraid that you would laugh at me. Now I have a real desire to see this woman, just to test her powers. The moment I read her advertisement in this morning's paper, I had a strong presentiment that she could help me out of my troubles, and I determined to visit her. See, here we are, right at the door, No. 50 Clark street. Won't you go up with me while I get my fortune told, Miss Seaton?"

"Oh, certainly; if you really wish to try your fortune, to-day is as good a time as any other."

They therefore ascended to Madam Lucille's rooms and rang a bell at the reception-room door. The sable usher immediately admitted them and asked them to be seated for a short time, as Madam was engaged at that moment. He then left them alone, while he went to inquire how soon they could have an audience with the great sibyl. Having told Mrs. Warne who her visitors were, the usher hurried over to my office and informed me. I instantly called my stenographer, and we proceeded quickly to the back room, where we took our seats behind the curtain.

A lady was already in Mrs. Warne's room, but she was easily dismissed with instructions to return next day. When she retired, Mrs. Thayer was admitted, and Miss Seaton wished to follow, but this could not be allowed, as only one could have an audience at a time. Mrs. Thayer entered the room with her veil down; and, what with her nervousness and the superstitious terror inspired by the weird appearance of the room, she was hardly able to walk to the visitor's chair. When she became somewhat accustomed to the peculiar light, she saw Madam Lucille standing beside the table. Her tall, commanding figure struck Mrs. Thayer with awe, and

Mrs. Warne already felt sure of drawing out everything that she knew.

"Come hither, my daughter," said Lucille, in a clear, sweet voice.

Mrs. Thayer advanced falteringly, and sank into the large chair which the sibyl pointed out.

"What would you know, my child?" continued Lucille. "State your errand quickly; as my time is short, to unfold the mysteries of the future. Like the Wandering Jew, I must forever advance upon my mission. What do you seek to know?"

Lucille's powerful mind, aided by her fantastic surroundings, had gained a complete ascendency over Mrs. Thayer's superstitious nature; in a voice trembling with emotion, she replied:

"I have come to learn my future."

"Then you must unveil; I can tell you nothing until I see your face," said Lucille.

Mrs. Thayer slowly removed her veil and sat motionless, regarding the fortune-teller as a frightened bird watches a snake.

"You wish to know your destiny, do you?" asked Lucille, gently. "Well, I can tell it, if the stars are propitious; but I must first look at your hand."

She paused and waved her wand with several mysterious gestures over Mrs. Thayer's head; then she swept forward and took her hand.

"Tell me the day and hour of your birth," continued Lucille.

"I was born about daybreak on the eighteenth of

October, 1816, replied Mrs. Thayer; "I cannot tell you the exact hour."

"That will be sufficiently accurate for the present," said Lucille; "though it may cause me much trouble in casting your horoscope."

Lucille continued to examine the lines of the hand, and presently commenced speaking in a low, but clear voice:

"Your parents are dead, and also one brother; your father passed through great dangers safely—ah! I see, he was a sailor. You have been surrounded by other sea-faring people; still, I cannot certainly tell what relationship they bore to you. I shall learn all when I cast your horoscope. Your father acquired moderate wealth, of which you have received your share; but you desire more, and you are not too scrupulous as to how you get it. Why, what means this?" she exclaimed, starting back and fixing a piercing glance on the cowering woman before her. "You are in danger! Yes; there is danger all about you, but it is impossible to tell now how it will end. There is a man in your trouble, who claims to love you; and there is a woman who comes between you. Ah! what is she doing!" she suddenly demanded in tragical tones, starting back with a look of terror in her eyes.

Mrs. Thayer fell back as if stabbed to the heart, and her whole attitude denoted guilty fear. Lucille, fearing that she would faint, handed her a glass of water, which soon revived her strength.

As soon as Mrs. Thayer had sufficiently recovered,

"Death!" shrieked Mrs. Thayer, and then she fell back lifeless."

Lucille again took her hand and carefully examined it; she then continued:

"I cannot do much now, but you must come again, when I have more time; then I will cast your horoscope, and will be able to tell you all you can wish to know ——" Breaking off suddenly, she changed her tone and demanded imperiously: "Who is this woman? Is she his enemy, or yours? *Are you sure that man loves you?*"

"Oh! yes; I am sure he does," Mrs. Thayer replied, hastily.

"Then what is the trouble between you and this woman?" asked Lucille. "She is older than you, yet she constantly crosses your path." Then, closing her eyes, Lucille broke out passionately and rapidly, like a person in a trance: "Why does she act so? What is the matter with her? She is often interfering with you, but is always followed by that man; he must be her enemy. See! a shadow falls over her! What does it mean! She fades away and vanishes — *it must be death!*"

"Death!" shrieked Mrs. Thayer, and then she fell back lifeless.

Lucille did everything possible to revive her visitor, but it was some minutes before she recovered sufficiently to be able to stand alone. She finally joined Miss Seaton, but promised to call the next day to have her horoscope read. She left a fee of ten dollars for the prepayment of the labor which Lucille would be forced to perform in reading the stars. When Miss Seaton and Mrs. Thayer left the room, the latter was scarcely able to walk, so much was she agitated and alarmed. They reached their boarding house in safety, however, and Mrs. Thayer at once retired to her room.

A large crowd of visitors had already assembled in Madam Lucille's reception room, so that there seemed to be a fair prospect that all the expenses of the affair would be paid out of the fortune-teller's receipts. Indeed, from the very first, Mrs. Warne had a great many more callers than she could attend to; but, by granting each one a short interview on the first day, long enough to learn what information they desired, it was an easy matter to satisfy them all to an exceptional extent. I put two good detectives at work to find out everything possible about the parties making the inquiries, and Lucille was thus able to astonish them with the accuracy of her knowledge as to the past. Of course, she was at liberty to exercise her own judgment as to her predictions for the future, since no one could tell whether they would prove true or not.

When every one had gone, Mrs. Warne changed her dress and returned to my office, where we had a hearty laugh over the superstitious folly of the many ladies who had consulted her. She told me many amusing secrets, which her fair visitors had confided to her, and I learned that some of the most fashionable people in the city had invoked her aid. She was rather fatigued by her labors, however, as the weather was warm, and the atmosphere of her room, at times, became almost suffocating. She said that she had made an engagement to admit Mrs. Thayer the first one, the next morning.

"Very well," said I, "you have succeeded in startling her very much indeed, and to-morrow you will be able to do much more. Be careful, however, to warn her against informing any one else of what you have told her, until her whole future is determined. It will not do to have her alarm Pattmore."

" I will caution her particularly on that point," replied Mrs. Warne; " I think I understand pretty well about how far I can go without terrifying her too much. I will send for Miss Seaton, and learn how Mrs. Thayer has acted since visiting me."

In the afternoon, Captain Sumner came in and asked what steps I had taken in his case. I told him that I could not tell him what I had done, nor what I was doing; but he could rest assured that the best talent I had was employed in his behalf; if everything worked as I hoped, I should accomplish the object which he sought, inside of a month.

"Well," he replied, I should like to take Annie back to Springfield as soon as possible; for I fear that she is again losing her health, and for the last day or two, she has been quite ill. Yesterday she received a letter from Pattmore, which I tried to snatch from her; but she was too quick for me, and I obtained only a small part of it. Here it is," he continued, showing me the lower corner of a letter; "see how he signs himself."

I took the fragment and saw the same signature as that which Pattmore had used in his former letters : "Your affectionate husband." The Captain went on :

" My blood got up when I read this, and I told her that if she ever saw Pattmore again, I would shoot them both; that I would no longer permit her to disgrace our family. Then she also flew into a violent passion, and said that she loved Pattmore, and that he intended to marry her when he next came to Chicago. As usual, she finally succeeded in appeasing my anger, and she promised to leave Pattmore forever. I also agreed to make my will in her favor, and we thus became friends again. I may now be able to get her away, as she has promised to go as soon as she is able; but I can easily destroy my will, if she refuses to keep her promise. What do you think about it?"

"Well, it can't do much harm, I guess, for you are probably in no particular danger just now."

"Then I will make my will to-day. By-the-by, there is a great fortune-teller in town; have you seen her advertisement?"

"Yes," I replied; "but there is nothing unusual in that. You can find such people here at all times."

"I know that," said the Captain; "but they are generally mere humbugs, while this one appears to be of a different class. She has been in the East Indies, and the fortune-tellers there are not humbugs, as I know by experience. I shall go to see her to-morrow. I had my fortune told once by a Hindoo in Calcutta, and he was correct in every particular as far as he went."

After the Captain had gone away, I sent for Mrs. Warne and told her that she would receive a visit from the Captain next day, and that she could learn all about his past history by referring to the conversation which my stenographer had taken down some time before. I then looked over a report I had just received from Miller, who was still watching Pattmore in Greenville. There was little of importance in it except an account of a conversation

between Miller and Pattmore, in which the latter said that
he was staking everything upon the hope of getting the
congressional nomination; if he should fail in that, he
would not remain in Greenville, but would go to Kansas
to live. Miller added that Pattmore received letters daily
from Mrs. Thayer.

I immediately wrote to Miller to secure a copy of one
of Mrs. Thayer's letters; and, if possible, to intercept
every one of them. I felt confident that she would describe her visit to the fortune-teller in part, at least, and
I was anxious to know how much she would reveal to
him. Besides if he were disposed to be superstitious, he
would probably be more or less affected by her account,
and I might use the knowledge thus gained, to good
advantage.

Late in the evening, Miss Seaton came in and told Mrs.
Warne that Mrs. Thayer had been greatly agitated by her
interview with Lucille; that she had shown great dejec-
tion and grief all the way home; and that she had immediately retired to her room, where she had thrown herself
on the bed; that she had risen, late in the evening, and
had written a very·long letter, which she had asked Miss
Seaton to put in the post-office for her, being too weak to
go out herself. Of course, Miss Seaton gave the letter to
Mrs. Warne, who immediately brought it to me. I opened
it at once and hastily read it through. It began, "My
dear husband," and went on to describe her visit to Lucille. She gave a full account of all that Lucille had said,
and also related the effect which the fortune-teller's revelations had had upon her. She said significantly that
Pattmore could understand how much she had been

alarmed by the references to the woman who came between them, for the inference was that Lucille meant
Mrs. Pattmore. However, she was going, she said, to
have her full fortune told the following day, and she would
write all about it in her next letter.

I had the letter copied and sent to the post-office in
time for the first mail.

CHAPTER IX.

I HAD sent word to my New York correspondent to make a thorough search for Henry Thayer, as I wished to learn definitely whether he was alive or dead. By communicating with the London board of underwriters, my agent learned that Henry Thayer was in command of an English whaler in the South Sea. At the latest advices from him, he was nearly ready to sail for England, as he needed only a few more whales to complete his cargo. I received this information the morning after Mrs. Thayer's first visit to Lucille, and I communicated the news to Mrs. Warne at once, instructing her to make the best possible use of it in her coming interview with Mrs. Thayer.

Shortly before ten o'clock the next morning, I took my place behind the curtain. In a few minutes Mrs. Thayer and Miss Seaton arrived, and Mrs. Thayer was promptly admitted to Lucille's presence. She removed her veil and sank into the visitor's chair with an expression half of longing and half of dread. Again Lucille waved her snaky wand, and, as before, the room was filled with the fumes of burning incense. Lucille looked at Mrs. Thayer's face intently, and said:

"My child, I am pleased to see you; I have worked at your horoscope unremittingly, but it is not completed to my satisfaction. There is some peculiar influence about you which prevents a clear reading of your future. Even your past, though much of it is easily determined, seems obscured by strange inconsistencies — not to say impossibilities. Some of the results were so startling as to make it necessary for me to refuse to reveal them, until, by a second test, I can decide whether there was no mistake in the solution of certain calculations. To-night, therefore, I shall do what rarely is necessary in reading the horoscope of ordinary humans — I must invoke the aid of my progenitor and master, Hermes. It is a dreadful task; one for which I must nerve myself to meet the greatest dangers and the most frightful scenes; but I never shrink from the path of duty, and I have confidence that the sanctity of my mission will give me safe conduct, even through the hosts of demons who must be met before I can come face to face with the great Egyptian king."

Lucille spoke with a weird earnestness, and a far-away look in her eyes, as if she actually realized the presence of ghouls and goblins. Mrs. Thayer fairly shivered with terror, but said nothing, and Lucille continued:

"I wish I dared read the whole of the horoscope as it was divulged to me in the lone watches of last night; but I have decided to omit all those portions where there is a possibility that the malign spirits around you have misinterpreted your past and future. When you were younger, you passed your days in happiness; you were very handsome, and you could charm the hearts of men without difficulty. There has been with you frequently, during your past years, a man some years older than yourself. He appears to have been a sailor; and, though

often away from you, he has always sought you out on
his return. He loves you, and is undoubtedly your true
friend; he is unmarried, yet he does not wish to make
you his wife. He wears a peculiar ring which he obtained
in the East Indies. He often consults this ring, and it
informs him whether he is in danger or the reverse. You
do not love this sailor as well as he loves you, and he
wishes to remove you from the other man. I cannot
understand the actions of the woman whom I mentioned
yesterday; I cannot tell whether she is living or dead.
The man you love has been with her; he gave her something in a spoon which she was forced to take. Ah! I
see! it was a medicine, a white powder — and now begins
the obscurity. Further on, I see that he visited you;
you ran to meet him and plied him with caresses. If he
were your husband it would partly clear away the cloud.
Is it so?"

"Yes," Mrs. Thayer at length replied, "he is my
husband."

"Well, that removes much of the uncertainty; this
woman loved that man and wished to keep him away
from you; he gave her a powder to make her sleep, so
that he could escape from her."

Then, suddenly catching Mrs. Thayer's hand, Lucille
glanced over it rapidly, and again closely examined the
chart. Drawing back from Mrs. Thayer, she eyed her
sternly and disapprovingly.

"Who is this other man?" she asked; "he, too, is a
sailor; he is handsome; he is brave; he is an officer;
yes, he commands a ship. He has been much with you,
but he is now far away. You loved him once, but now

the other man has come between you." Then, pausing a moment, she broke forth rapidly and harshly : "Woman, you have tried to deceive me ! This sea captain is your husband !"

Mrs. Thayer was only able to say, as she fell back, fainting :

"He is dead ! he is ——"

Lucille soon revived her, and then asked whether she was strong enough to hear the remainder of her fortune. Mrs. Thayer signified her assent, and Lucille again examined the chart. She first said :

"You cannot deceive me; your husband is away at sea; is it not so ?"

"He *was* my husband," said Mrs. Thayer, in a half audible voice; "but he went away several years ago, and I heard that he was dead. I had fallen in love with the other man, and, on hearing of my husband's death, I married the man I loved. It can't be possible that Henry is alive."

"Yes, he is," replied Lucille; "and I think he is about to return to seek for you; but the horoscope again becomes obscure. It is as I feared; the only means of learning the truth will be through the aid of the dread Hermes, whose power no demon can resist. To-morrow you shall learn all that my art can discover about your past and your future."

"But can you tell me no more than this to-day?" asked Mrs. Thayer, in a vexed tone. "You have given me only bad news. How long shall I live and be happy with my husband ?"

"That man is not your husband, and you cannot long

live happily with him.   As far as the cloud permits me to
see, I can discern that something terrible is about to
happen to him.   You are in danger yourself; there seems
to be a strange fatality attending your fate wherever it
comes in contact with that man; it is especially gloomy
when complicated by tbe presence of the other woman.
As I have before told you, I cannot clearly see from this
horoscope what will be your *absolute* future; but I can
tell you this much: — and, woman, weigh well my words,
for the spirit of prophecy is strong within me — your
future is dependent upon your present decision.   Fate is
unchangeable, and neither seer nor sibyl can alter its
least decree; but it is sometimes permitted to us to determine the *contingent* future of a person and no more.   We
then say, thus and thus has been the past; the future
may be thus, or it may be so; one course of conduct
now, will lead to *this* result; the other will lead to *that.*
Yours is such a horoscope; and, even with the aid of my
mighty master, I cannot expect to do anything more than
to learn definitely the two alternatives which are to be
presented to you, and the consequence of your decision
each way.   To-morrow I will see you again at an early
hour, and will tell you all I have learned during the
night."

"Can you tell me no more now?" demanded Mrs.
Thayer, impatiently.   "Is it then true that my first
husband is alive?"

"It is true," replied Lucille; "and he is at present
commanding a ship far away in the South Sea, which is
the reason why you could not find him."

14

" How do you know that I ever looked for him ?" said Mrs. Thayer, languidly.

" No; you did not look for him; but the other sailor who loves you, made inquiries for a long time. I see him plainer now; he must be your brother."

Mrs. Thayer had been very much awed by the imposing manners of Lucille, and by the mystic surroundings in which she was placed. She was now quite in Lucille's power, and I should have proceeded to force her to reveal the truth about Pattmore's crime, had she been stronger physically; but I was afraid to test her endurance too far in one day. I had arranged, a series of simple signals, which would not attract the attention of any one but Lucille, and I therefore signalled to her that she might close the interview. Mrs. Thayer lifted her head to look at Lucille a few moments after the latter had spoken of her brother, and said :

" You are the strangest woman I have ever met. You have told me things which I believed were known only by myself. All that you have said is the truth; but you do not tell me enough. I wish to know what I must do to make amends for all the wrong I have done. I have been very wicked, I know."

" If you really wish to do right, there is still a prospect that you may be happy. My duty is to show you that you are doing wrong, and to help you to change your course of action."

" Will you not tell me about my—"

Mrs. Thayer could not complete the sentence, but she evidently meant Pattmore, so Lucille said :

" Yes, my child; I will tell you all to-morrow; but I

think you are unable to bear more at present. I will point out two paths, and will show you where each one of them leads: then, if you wish, I will give you my advice; after that, all will depend upon yourself. You can be happy again, if you decide to follow my counsel."

"Indeed, I will try to do so," replied Mrs. Thayer. "I have suffered myself to be led astray; but, hereafter, I will be guided by you. I never before heard a fortune-teller who could talk as you do,—you give such good advice."

"I endeavor to use my powers for the good of mankind," said Lucille, solemnly. "I speak only what I know to be true. When I have told you all, you must decide upon your course; and, if you choose the right one, you will, doubtless, be very happy. Be careful that you do not reveal to any one the knowledge you have this day learned from me; when you have heard all, you can tell as much as you please. Farewell, my child; be here promptly at ten o'clock to-morrow, for my time is precious."

Mrs. Thayer withdrew, joined Miss Seaton in the reception room, and they returned home. Lucille then received in rapid succession the visitors who had made appointments the previous day. She had a note-book filled with information obtained by my detectives, and she was thus enabled to satisfy them all immediately; or else, to postpone telling their fortunes until the next day. Then the new arrivals were admitted long enough to tell what they wished to know, after which they each received appointments for the next day. When all were disposed of, Lucille came into the back room to change her dress. I congratulated her upon her success, and was about to withdraw with my stenographer, when the usher came in and said that a gentleman desired an audience. From his description, I felt confident that Captain Sumner was the person who had arrived. I therefore begged Lucille to give him a full sitting, and to read his past for him very thoroughly.

"By the way," I added, "you recollect that while he was away at sea, his sweetheart, Miss Curtis, married a wealthy New York banker, named Agnew. Well, I saw a notice the other day of the death of a banker of that name in New York, and I feel sure that his old flame is now a widow. I want you to refer to this fact in telling his future."

"Oh! well," said Lucille, with some vexation, "I'm rather tired of the business already, and I don't care to spend the whole afternoon in that hot room; so I shall get rid of him as soon as he is satisfied. If you want to tell me anything, make a sound like the gnawing of a rat, and I will come out."

Accordingly, I resumed my place at the door, with my stenographer close beside me, and the Captain was ushered into Lucille's room. She motioned to him to be seated, and then asked, in her most commanding tones:

"What can you learn from Lucille that you have not already learned from the Hindoo of Calcutta?"

The Captain regarded her for an instant in reverent amazement; but, finally, he said:

"I see that you know my past, and that you are truly one of those who can read the fate of others. I am in trouble, and I wish to know when I shall escape from it, if ever. The Hindoo told me much, but I would know more."

Without further conversation, except to ask the day and hour of his birth, Lucille proceeded to pore over a chart and to examine his hand. Finally, she gazed at him steadily a few minutes, and said:

"What I have to say is the truth alone; if it be painful to you, it is because the truth is not always pleasant. Listen calmly, therefore, to the words which the stars declare to be true: Your parents are both dead; your father was a sea-captain, and he brought you up in the same profession. On one of his cruises, a Sepoy presented him with three rings, one of which you now wear; its powers are very great, and it has frequently rendered you important services; take care that you lose it not. It has even saved your life. Yes," she continued, after closely examining the palm of his left hand; "your life has been attempted three separate times lately. You have two sisters living; one of them is happily married and lives in comfort in an eastern State; the other married a sea-captain, but she does not live with her husband. She is with you, and is in poor health. Why! is it possible!" she exclaimed, suddenly. "It was your sister who made the attempt on your life! You may not suspect that your young and charming sister, whom you so deeply love, could have been guilty of such an act; but, unless my powers have failed me so that I cannot read the stars aright, such is the fact. Wait; lest I should have made a mistake, I will try again. It seems too horrible to be believed."

The Captain had buried his face in his hands; but now he looked up and said:

"It is unnecessary to try again; you are right. I see that you are one of the gifted ones of this world, and I wish you to tell me all; I can bear it."

Lucille continued her examination of the Captain's hand as she went on speaking:

"Your sister still has the same kind of poison with her which she used before. She does not intend to use it herself — she has no motive for committing suicide; but she may intend to give it to you again. You must be careful, for that is your greatest danger. Your principal trouble for some time has been caused by that sister. She no longer loves her husband, who has wholly disappeared from your knowledge, and she professes to believe that he is dead. This is not the case, however: he is now in command of an English whaling ship in the South Sea, and he will soon return to England."

At this, the Captain sprang up in a whirl of excitement and joy. In relating the story to me the next day, he said that he felt like taking Lucille in his arms and giving her a genuine sailor hug; but she looked so fierce and wicked that he got the idea that she was a genuine witch; and he was afraid that her beautiful white hands would turn into claws, and that she would soon make a meal of him, if she felt so disposed.

When he sat down again, Lucille again scanned the chart and compared it with his hand. She seemed very much disturbed at the revelations, and, at length, she said:

"Your troubles are so closely interwoven with those of

your sister that I cannot separate them; but I never saw a horoscope so full of frightful scenes — I do not wish to go on with it."

"Please do not stop," said the Captain; "I feel that you have the power to tell me all, and I must know it. I will pay you anything you ask," he added, taking out a roll of money.

"My fees are invariable," said Lucille, drawing herself up haughtily. "You insult me by suggesting that I need to be paid extra to tell the truth."

"I beg your pardon," replied the Captain excitedly; "but I hope you will not refuse to tell me all you know. I can bear it, I assure you."

"Know then that your sister is deeply in love with a very bad man, who lives two or three hundred miles from here. She became acquainted with him in the East and he seduced her, though he was a married man, living with his lawful wife. To quiet your sister's scruples, he had a marriage ceremony performed; but, of course, it had no legal value, since both of the parties were already married. She became *enceinte* by this man, and she caused the premature removal of the evidence of her shame by an abortion. This crime you connived at, though you did not advise it. But the worst is not yet told: this wicked man, finding that you were determined to prevent him from seeing your sister, *resolved to murder his wife*, and to marry your sister legally, supposing that her husband was dead. He accomplished part of his design by poisoning his wife; but he has not yet been able to carry out the whole of his plan. He is now in danger, but he knows it not. He will soon be arrested and tried for murder. If you can succeed in uniting your sister and her lawful husband, they may be able to forget the past and live together happily. All, however, depends upon her. At present she is in deep distress, but the effect of it will be good for her. There is a strong hope that she may be led to see the character of her wicked lover in its true light, and that she may return penitently to the arms of her husband, if he will receive her."

" Oh! he will, I know he will," said the Captain.

" Then, when that happens, your troubles will be at an end. Now I can tell you but little more, as I have a great task to perform, and I must be left alone."

On hearing Lucille say this, I immediately gave the signal, as agreed, and she made an excuse to leave the room for a moment.

" What more do you want ?" she asked.

" You have forgotten to tell him about his old sweetheart, Mrs. Agnew."

"Oh! let me skip that," said Lucille impatiently, " I am nearly exhausted, and I cannot stand the atmosphere of that room much longer."

" Just tell the Captain about Mrs. Agnew, and then you will be through work for the day. Try to send him off happy," I pleaded.

" Oh! yes; that is always the way : provided the Captain goes away happy, you dcn't care what becomes of me. Well, I suppose I must ; but I will never undertake such a *role* again."

When Lucille returned to the Captain, he was sitting with his face buried in his hands; but he looked up instantly and asked whether she had anything more to tell him.

She looked at the chart for a few minutes and then said :

"In your youth, you loved a lady of great beauty, and she returned your love; but while you were away at sea, her parents made her believe that you were false to her. They wished her to marry a wealthy banker, and, in a fit of pique, she accepted him. She has always loved you in secret, however, and now that her husband is dead —"

"Is that so?" ejaculated the Captain, springing up in great delight.

"Yes," replied Lucille; "he died a short time ago, and she is now passing her widowhood in New York. She is stouter than she was, but she is still handsome, and she has never ceased to love you. This completes the reading of your horoscope."

The Captain rose to go, but paused to express his feelings. He spoke slowly and with great emotion, since Lucille had completely secured his confidence.

"Madam, I thank you from my heart for the revelations you have made to me. I know that most of the things you have told me are true, and I am satisfied of the truth of the rest also. I should like to pay you in proportion to the value of your words to me." So saying he went out quickly, leaving one hundred dollars on the table.

I found that Lucille's fame was becoming uncomfortably great, since the reception-room was thronged with eager inquirers, who insisted on seeing her, even after the close of her office hours. I, therefore, arranged with Mr. Bangs, my general superintendent, to have a crowd of my own *employees* constantly in attendance, so that outsiders, seeing so many others waiting for an audience, would not remain. By this means, Lucille was able thereafter, to receive as many, or as few, as she chose, and her labors were greatly lightened.

CHAPTER X.

AFTER the interview with Lucille, Mrs. Thayer returned to her boarding-house with Miss Seaton, and invited the latter to spend the day with her. She said that she was low-spirited and wanted company to keep off the "blues." She was very nervous, and she could not take an interest in anything. She said several times that Lucille was the most wonderful person she had ever met, and that she had heard things which convinced her of Lucille's supernatural powers; but she carefully avoided stating anything definite relative to the revelations made to her. Finally she commenced to write a long letter, and Miss Seaton became absorbed in a novel.

After some time the Captain came in, looking very solemn, and Miss Seaton saw that he wished to have a private talk with Mrs. Thayer. Accordingly she rose to leave the room, remarking that she was going down town in the evening and would like to have Mrs. Thayer accompany her. Miss Seaton knew that it was very improbable that Mrs. Thayer would go, on account of the fatigue and excitement of the morning; but she hoped that the latter would give her the letter to put in the post-office. On hearing the approach of the Captain, Mrs. Thayer had hastily concealed her writing materials, thus showing that she was writing to Pattmore. On entering her own room, Miss Seaton took a seat close by a door which connected the two rooms. This door was nailed up and the cracks had been filled with cotton; but she quickly pulled out the filling and obtained an excellent opening to hear all the conversation in the next room.

The Captain first asked his sister when she would be ready to return to Springfield with him. She replied that she would go as soon as she felt able to stand the journey.

"Annie," said he, in an impressive manner, "I fear that you are deceiving me, and that you intend to do me harm. Why do you seek my life? You know that I have done all I could for you, and that I will continue to do so. Why, then, do you wish to poison me? I know that you have poison with you, and that I am the only one for whom it can be intended."

"No, no, you are wrong," replied Mrs. Thayer, in trembling tones; "you are my brother, and why should I wish to injure you?"

"Annie, I know that you have poison about you," said the Captain, firmly, "and I am afraid to remain with you any longer. I have forgiven you once, but now it is my duty to cast you off; *you are plotting to take my life.*"

"Who told you this? What reason have I given you for thinking so?" demanded Mrs. Thayer.

"I have been to see a wonderful fortune-teller, who ——"

The words had no more than passed her lips, when he was interrupted by an exclamation of terror and surprise from Mrs. Thayer, who started to her feet and then fell back upon the sofa, fainting. The Captain was much alarmed at the effect of his remark, and he could not understand why she had fainted at the mere mention of the source of his information. However, he did not spend any time in trying to account for her terror; his first action was to bathe her temples with cold water, in order to restore her to consciousness. When she had partly revived, she lay on the sofa with her eyes closed, as if she had no strength left. Finally she spoke in a weak voice, without looking at her brother:

"Was it a fortune-teller who told you what you have just accused me of?"

"Yes," replied the Captain, "and I know that she speaks the truth."

"My God!" exclaimed Mrs. Thayer, "how could that woman have known that? Well, it is true that I have some poison, though, as God is my judge, it was not meant for you; but, I was resolved that if I could not escape from my present misery, I would take it myself. Never, for an instant, did I intend it for you."

"In either case, Annie, I must have the poison."

Mrs. Thayer rose with great effort, and, going to her trunk, produced a small package labeled "POISON," in conspicuous letters. She handed it to the Captain, and he said:

"I will now destroy this package and thus remove all temptation from you; let us both thank God that you have been prevented from carrying out your design. O, Annie! may this be the last time that I ever shall have reason to doubt you. The fortune-teller whom I mentioned is a wonderful woman. I learned from her many

things which I will tell you when you are strong enough
to hear them."

"I should like you to tell me very much," said Mrs.
Thayer, eagerly; "perhaps she could tell my fortune, if
I should visit her."

"Yes, indeed; she could tell you all your past and
future; you ought to go there."

"Well, I guess I will try to go to-morrow, if I am
strong enough," said Mrs. Thayer.

The Captain kissed her tenderly, and said:

"Annie, never again follow the advice of an evil coun-
sellor; you will never be happy while you continue in a
path which you know to be wrong. The fortune-teller
had good news for us both, and all will go well if you will
only be guided by the wishes of your true friends, who
love you and who desire to save you from sorrow."

The Captain then went out and left Mrs. Thayer dozing
on the sofa.

In the evening, after supper, Miss Seaton went to Mrs.
Thayer's room to see whether the latter wished to take a
walk. Mrs. Thayer was not able to go out, but she asked
Miss Seaton to put a letter in the post-office for her.
Miss Seaton took the letter and brought it straight to Mrs.
Warne, who delivered it to me at once. I opened it and
read it aloud to my stenographer, who took down its
contents as fast as the words fell from my lips.

The letter contained a full account of Mrs. Thayer's
second visit to Lucille, and it betrayed great fear of dis-
covery and punishment. She said that she had thought
their secret to be perfectly safe, but now she knew that
there was at least one person who could disclose their

guilt to the world, since that person had the power of finding out everything. She begged him to come to Chicago, to see Lucille, and have his fortune told; he would then learn the wonderful extent of her powers, and would be able to decide what was the best course to .pursue. She thought he ought to fly for safety at once, since the fortune-teller predicted that he was in great danger. As for herself, she expected to go East soon, as her brother was anxious to start. If Pattmore did not come to Chicago immediately she might never see him again; she could not bear the idea of separation, but she knew that it must come. It was evident that Mrs. Thayer had wholly forgotten Lucille's injunction to maintain silence upon the subject of her revelations, and I debated an instant whether I should send the letter; but I finally decided to let it go, as he would receive it too late to interfere with my plans, even if he should come to Chicago. I sent a letter to Miller by the same mail, telling him to keep a strict watch on Pattmore, as I feared that he might leave Greenville suddenly. In case of such a movement Miller must telegraph to me instantly.

Miller's reports for several days had been to the effect that Pattmore was working very hard to secure the Congressional nomination, but that he seemed very much troubled about some other matter. He had changed his mind about going West, and had asked Miller to go to Galveston, Texas, with him, in case he failed to get the nomination. Although he still had hosts of friends, he did not confide his plans to any one except Miller. This showed me that there would be but little probability that Pattmore would come to Chicago without Miller's knowledge. That same evening Miller sent me a telegram stating that Pattmore had just received a long letter, evidently from Mrs. Thayer; on reading it he had shown great excitement, and had afterwards become gloomy and dejected to an unusual degree. Miller wished to know whether I had any special instructions about the letter. As this was the letter which Miss Seaton had secured the day before, I replied that he need not trouble himself about it, but that he must keep a close watch upon Pattmore, and endeavor to retain him in Greenville as long as possible.

By the early mail next morning I received a letter from Dr. Stuart, of Greenville; having finished the work upon which he had been engaged, he had begun the analysis of Mrs. Pattmore's bowels; he said that he would let me know the result within a few days.

The whole affair was now gradually drawing to a focus, and I felt confident of a successful termination. I therefore instructed Mrs. Warne to describe me to Mrs. Thayer, and to say that I was watching her movements constantly.

About nine o'clock that morning Mrs. Thayer went out as usual with Miss Seaton, and they proceeded straight to Lucille's rooms. They were the first arrivals, and Mrs. Thayer was admitted to Lucille's presence at once; but Miss Seaton immediately went back to her boarding-house, as I wished to have Mrs. Thayer return home alone. Mrs. Thayer was in a more impressionable state than ever before. The day was dark and lowering, showing every sign of an approaching storm; outside there had been the noisy bustle of active business life, while within the limits of Lucille's mystic chamber all was hushed in a deathly silence. The monotonous swinging of the lamps, the perfume-laden air, the ghastly skeletons, and the imperious bearing and powerful will of Lucille—all struck upon her imagination with resistless force. As she sank into the seat which Lucille pointed out, she felt like a criminal entering the prisoner's dock for trial. She felt that she must relieve herself from her load of guilt or she would forever suffer the torments of remorse.

"Well, my child," said Lucille, in her most solemn tones, "to-day you have come to learn all, and I trust that you have nerved yourself to sustain the revelations which I have to make. I have been through many difficulties and terrible dangers since I last saw you, and a very sad story has been laid before me. Your situation is one of great peril, and upon your own decision this day will rest your hopes of happiness hereafter. Still, you must not be cast down; if you will only resolve to do what is right, your sorrows will gradually pass away, while health and happiness will steadily return to you. Your worst crime was the destruction of your unborn child, for that was a sin against nature herself; but true repentance will save you from the effects of that sin, further than you have already suffered."

This was the first time Lucille had mentioned the fact that she knew of the abortion; yet it seemed perfectly natural to Mrs. Thayer that Lucille should know it; hence, beyond turning very pale at the memory of her suffering, she did not manifest any special emotion on hearing Lucille's words.

15

The sibyl continued speaking as she gazed, first at Mrs. Thayer's hand, and then at the chart:

"This man, whom you so wrongly love, does not return you the affection of a true husband; he loves you only for selfish, sensual purposes; he will fondle you as a plaything for a few years, and then he will cast you off for a younger and more handsome rival, even as he has already put away his first wife for your sake. If you do not give him up now, some day he will throw you aside or trample you under foot. Think you he will fear to do in the future what he has done in the past? When he wearies of you, have you any doubt that he will murder you *as he has already murdered his wife?*"

Lucille had spoken in a rapid, sibilant whisper, leaning forward so as to bring her eyes directly before Mrs. Thayer's face, and the effect was electrical. Mrs. Thayer struggled for a moment, as if she would rise, and then fell back and burst into tears. This was a fortunate relief, since she would have fainted if she had not obtained some mode of escape for her pent-up feelings. Seeing that there was no further danger of overpowering Mrs. Thayer, as long as she was able to cry, Lucille continued:

"Yes, the heartless villain murdered his wife by poisoning her. I can see it all as it occurred; it is a dreadful scene, yet I know that it must be true—a woman of middle age is lying in bed; she has evidently been very handsome, but now she shows signs of a long illness; your lover, her husband, enters, and he wishes to give her some medicine; but see, she motions him away, though she is unable to speak; she must know that he is going to poison her; yet she cannot help herself, and the nurse does not suspect his design. Now he has given her the poison, and she is writhing in an agony of pain. He professes to be much afflicted, and, oh, heavens! with the treachery of Judas, he attempts to kiss her! Now it is all over; with one last, reproachful look, she has passed to that land where 'the wicked cease from troubling, and the weary are at rest.' She is dead, *and her husband is her murderer.*"

"Oh! for God's sake, spare me, spare me!" exclaimed Mrs. Thayer, between her sobs. "I cannot listen to the description of such a death-bed scene without horror. I know I have been very guilty, but I shall try to make amends in the future. Have pity on me, I beg of you, and do not overwhelm me with such terrible scenes."

"You must hear all," said Lucille, firmly. "There are two more acts in this tragedy to which you must listen; the first is a weird scene in a church-yard by night, and the clear starlight only half reveals the actors; there are three men engaged in digging at this woman's grave; yes, even in death, her body cannot rest in peace. Near by lies the corpse of another woman, whose cold, white face is turned up mutely to the silent stars; now the men reach the coffin and try to drag it from the grave. What is their object? Ah! I see! they wish to substitute one corpse for the other, so that the poison will never be discovered in case of an inquest upon the body of the murdered woman. Suddenly three other men rush upon the grave-diggers before they have been able to pull the coffin from the grave; a chase ensues, and pistol-shots are fired; but finally the resurrectionists escape, though they have been foiled in their purpose. The last scene is the inquest: the coffin is brought in, but the murderer dare not look upon the face of his victim; a sham investigation is held, and he is cleared by the verdict of the jury; but other watchful eyes have been regarding the proceedings; keen detectives have been at work, and they now step in, unknown to the public, and take quiet possession of the corpse; the stomach is removed for analysis, and a chemist of great reputation takes charge of it; poison has been found; positive proof of your lover's guilt have been obtained, and he will suffer the penalty of his crime. You also are in danger, but if you tell the truth, you will be saved."

As Lucille impetuously placed before Mrs. Thayer the occurrences which my investigations had disclosed, it seemed to the latter as if she were the victim of a horrible nightmare. She felt that she was surrounded by unseen foes, who were gradually tightening the toils in which she and Pattmore had become entangled. She was neither brave nor self-sacrificing; she had a sensitive dread of exposure, trial, and punishment, which was aggravated by a knowledge of guilt and an uncertainty as to the extent to which she had become legally liable; also, she had none of the spirit of devoted affection which sometimes prompts a woman to bear the greatest hardships for the sake of the man she loves; hence, she was ready to do anything to save herself, even at the expense of Pattmore's life. As Lucille concluded her terrible recital, Mrs. Thayer shrieked in an agony of remorse and fear:

"Oh, have mercy on me! I am lost! I am lost! Tell

me what I can do to escape punishment; I will obey you wholly—I will do anything you tell me. Oh, save me, save me! I know you can if you will."

It was some time before Lucille could restore her to a quiet state of mind, but at length her sobs ceased and Lucille continued :

"The worst is now past, and if you will return to your brother and confess all, he will forgive you. When you are called upon to tell what you know about this wicked man, you must do so without reserve. You will never see him again except in prison. If you do as your brother wishes, you will regain your light heart and sweet disposition; your real husband will come back to you, and your future will be one of happiness."

Mrs. Thayer sat motionless, with her face buried in her shawl; occasionally a long, choking sob would make her whole frame quiver, but otherwise she gave hardly a sign of life.

"Let me see your face," commanded Lucille.

As Mrs. Thayer slowly raised her tear-stained countenance, Lucille gazed intently into her eyes, and again examined the lines of her hand; then she went on speaking :

"There is another man near you, whose presence you do not suspect; neither have you ever seen him; but he is watching you all the time. You will soon meet him, for he wishes to talk with you. He is only of medium height, but he is very well built and powerful; he has a full face, ruddy complexion, brown hair, and gray eyes; he wears full whiskers all around his face, and his expression is kindly but resolute. He is a very deter-

mined man, and when he tries to do anything he never
gives up until he has accomplished his object. He has
great power, and if you follow his counsel he can save
you from harm; but you must trust him fully and tell
him the whole truth, for he can instantly detect any
falsehood or evasion, and he will be very dangerous to
you if you try to deceive him. This is all I have to tell
you at present, my child; I wish you well, but I cannot
devote more time to you. I hope you will give heed to
what I have told you, and that you will decide to follow
the right path. There are many now awaiting an audience with me, and I must hasten to admit them, since I
cannot tarry long in one city. I have been here now
some time, and I must soon journey on; the waste places
of the far West call to me—yea, even the deserts of the
barren hills. I must plunge into solitude for a time, to
commune with Nature."

Then, raising her arms, Lucille placed both hands
lightly on Mrs. Thayer's head and said, solemnly:

"May the Spirit of Eternal Truth go with thee, my
child, to guide thee forevermore! Farewell."

When Mrs. Thayer looked up, after a few minutes of
silence, Lucille had disappeared; having slipped into the
room where I and my stenographer were listening. Seeing that the fortune-teller had dismissed her, Mrs. Thayer
drew down her heavy veil and left the room. One of my
men was stationed at the front door to watch her movements, so that when I joined him, after a few minutes
hurried talk with Lucille, he pointed out to me the direction she had taken. I hastened down the street until I
caught sight of her; then, seeing that she was on her way

"She was struck almost speechless with fear. She could only ejaculate, Oh! God, help me! that man has come."

back to her boarding-house, I decided not to speak to her just then. The street was quite crowded, and I preferred not to risk having a scene in the presence of so many spectators. Therefore I walked at a safe distance behind her until she was across the bridge; but, on reaching a quiet neighborhood, I overtook her and said:

"Mrs. Thayer, I believe?"

It must be remembered that she had no acquaintances in Chicago except her fellow-boarders; hence my recognition of her would have startled her, even had she never been told to expect me. But, as it was, my appearance gave her a great shock, since she was at that moment revolving in her mind the information given her by Lucille. Therefore, when she was addressed by a stranger, whom she at once recognized as the man about whom Lucille had given her a forewarning, she was struck almost speechless with fear. She could only ejaculate:

"Oh! God help me! that man has come!"

I saw she was nearly ready to faint, so I took her arm and said:

"Mrs. Thayer, I wish you to accompany me to my office."

She was so weak that I supported her a short distance until one of my men, who had remained within call, could bring a hack. I then helped Mrs. Thayer into the carriage and told the driver to proceed at once to my office. Mrs. Thayer said nothing, and showed no objection to my wishes; but she was greatly alarmed, and she could not take her eyes off my face. She had a sort of helpless, questioning look, which I was glad to see, since it was evidence that she was now wholly under my control.

When the carriage stopped, I assisted her to walk up stairs into my private office, where my stenographer had already taken a position to hear without being seen. I gave her a comfortable chair, and handed her a glass of water, for I saw that she was very faint. As soon as her color began to show that she had revived I said :

"Mrs. Thayer, you perceive that I am well acquainted with you. I am sorry that you are in trouble, and I wish to be your friend, if you will allow me to be so; all I ask is that you tell me the whole truth about all your difficulties."

"Are you really my friend?" she asked, in a trembling voice; "can I rely upon what you say, and be sure that you will not take advantage of me? Oh, sir, my heart seems ready to break, and I know not what to think. I am a poor, weak woman, completely in your power."

"You need have no fear of me," I replied, "I know nearly everything relative to your troubles, but I wish you to tell me all the facts; then I shall know precisely what to do to help you. It is possible to raise a criminal charge against you, but it is my desire to prevent that; therefore, you must tell me everything, without any reservation whatever."

"Who are you?" she asked, after a few moments of thought. "You have not told me your name, yet I know you; I have heard of you before, and I know it will be useless for me to try to hide anything from you, but I would like to know your name."

"My name is Pinkerton," I answered, "but I cannot tell you how I know you, nor why I take an interest in your affairs. I wish you to give me a full account of your relations with Pattmore ever since your first acquaintance with him."

I then gave her a glass of wine to strengthen her, and asked her to proceed. As she spoke at first in a very low voice, I professed to be hard of hearing, in order that she should speak loud enough for my stenographer to hear also.

She first referred to her early married life, when she was perfectly happy in Henry's love; then she said that he made several very long voyages, and when he came home he remained only a few days each time. During one of these voyages, she met Pattmore and his wife in Brooklyn, and they became well acquainted. Afterward Pattmore frequently came to Brooklyn alone, and he always spent much of his time in her society. She did not realize the danger of his intercourse at first; but, gradually, he began to make love to her, and, finally, he accomplished her ruin. Thenceforward she was wholly under his control, especially after Henry's desertion of her. He brought her to his own hotel on the plea that she would be company for his wife, and she lived as his mistress, in fact, though not outwardly, until her brother came to take her away. Her brother succeeded in awakening her remorse, and she determined to return to Connecticut with him. Pattmore, however, opposed this action very strongly, and offered to marry her immediately, saying that his wife was sure to die soon from quick consumption, since all her family had died of that disease at about her age. They were therefore secretly married, and she then wrote to her brother that she should not return to Connecticut. When she discovered that she was *enceinte* she was much alarmed, and she again decided to return to her brother after the abortion had been performed, but Pattmore had a strong control over her still. As soon as she was able to go out, after her illness, Pattmore wrote to her to get a certain prescription put up by a druggist. She did so, and then sent the powders to him. In a short time Pattmore came to Chicago and told her that he had arranged to poison his wife. She was very much shocked at first, but he told her that Mrs. Pattmore could only live about a year anyhow, and that she would suffer a great deal during her rapid decline; hence he argued that there could be no harm in hastening her death to save her from many weeks of pain. He said that he had already commenced to poison her, using small doses, so as to break down her system gradually. While he was there Captain Sumner came back from the East, and he was very angry at Mrs. Thayer for permitting Pattmore to visit her. Then Pattmore told her to poison her brother in order that she might inherit his property. This proposition perfectly horrified her, as she really loved her brother; but Pattmore said that they never could live together as long as Captain Sumner was alive, and that he was afraid the Captain would some day get into a passion and kill them both. In this way he worked on her feelings until she agreed to give her brother some of the powder which she had sent to Greenville. Accordingly she made three attempts to poison her brother, but fortunately she was not successful. Pattmore then returned to Greenville, and soon afterward his wife died. He had visited her only once since that time. but they corresponded regularly. He was very guarded in his letters as to what he said about his wife's death, but she knew that he had carried out his plan, because he had told her so distinctly when he last saw her. He said that he had given her small doses every day until she died; but the doctor believed that she had died of dysentery, so that he was all safe.

When she had finished, I said:

"Well, Mrs. Thayer, I suppose you are aware that you are not legally Pattmore's wife?"

"Yes, I am," she said, with a sort of blind persistency; "his first wife is dead, and as I was legally married to him I am now his wife."

"No, Mrs. Thayer," I replied, "I will show you that your pretended marriage was no marriage at all; when it took place Pattmore's wife was alive, and he could not contract a second legal marriage; again, you have no evidence that your husband is dead, and it is therefore probable that you could not marry again legally. Hence, as he *certainly* committed bigamy, and as you *probably* have done the same, there could be no legal marriage between you."

"Yes, Mr. Pinkerton," she acknowledged, sadly, "I know you are right, but still I cling to that belief. If I could be sure that Henry was alive, I should not regard Pattmore as my husband; but, as his wife is dead, and Henry is also dead to me, I shall think that I am Pattmore's wife."

"Well, you can have your doubts set at rest very soon," said I, "for I have received letters from England saying that Henry is on his return from a whaling voyage in the South Sea."

"Is that so?" gasped Mrs. Thayer. "Well, I was told that, but I could hardly believe it. Oh, what shall I do? It was all my fault that Henry left me; he loved me truly, and I once loved him. Oh, if he would only forgive me, and love me, I might hope to be happy again; but I fear he can never pardon the wrongs I have done him."

"Do not despair, Mrs. Thayer," I said; "Henry may be willing to forgive and forget if you show yourself ready to return his affection. However, the first business is to circumvent Pattmore, and you must lend your assistance."

"What are you going to do with me?" she asked, in a timid voice.

"I shall let you go home," I replied; "but I shall keep a strict watch upon your actions, and if you show a spirit of true repentance, I will shield you from the penalties of your crimes. You will be called upon to testify in court against Pattmore, and then your brother will take you to his farm in Connecticut. You can go now, but your brother must come here and become responsible for your appearance when wanted. One thing more, Mrs. Thayer; you are receiving letters from Pattmore every day; now, I wish you to send me all his letters without opening or answering them. If you attempt to deceive me in anything I shall be obliged to put you in prison."

"Oh, no, no!" she said, eagerly; "you can trust me, I assure you, for I know that I am in your power; a fortune-teller told me so."

"Well, well, I don't care anything about fortune-tellers—I never saw one that wasn't a humbug—but you may depend upon it that I cannot be deceived, and I will not be trifled with. You can go home now and tell your brother to come over here to become your security."

So saying, I called a carriage and sent her home in charge of one of my men. On returning to my office, I found Mrs. Warne awaiting me. I complimented her very highly on her success, and told her that she need not continue the business of fortune-telling more than a day or two longer. I told her to be careful not to receive Mrs. Thayer again, however, but to instruct the usher to tell her that Madam Lucille never received any lady a second time after having completed her horoscope.

In about half an hour Captain Sumner came in. I told him that I was now master of the situation, and that I would make a decided move in a day or two.

"Yes," said the Captain, " Annie has told me a great deal, and she says that I must become responsible for her, and guarantee that she shall not leave town. How have you accomplished all this? I cannot understand it."

"Some day perhaps I will tell you all about it," I replied, " but I cannot do so just now. I wish you to bring your sister here to-morrow morning; I will prepare an affidavit for her to sign, and then we shall soon have Pattmore under arrest."

"Well, if you will only have him punished as he deserves," said the Captain, "I shall consider no reward too great for you. He is a snake in the grass, who has ruined my sister, and covered our family with shame. Now I want revenge."

"I shall do all in my power to have him punished," I said; " and I am very well pleased to see the end so near.

By the way, you might write to Mr. Chapman to inform him of our success."

"I will, indeed," said the Captain, enthusiastically; "if it had not been for him, I never should have thought of coming to you, Mr. Pinkerton."

"Well, good-day, Captain; come here with Mrs. Thayer about ten o'clock to-morrow morning."

I immediately placed the facts before my lawyer, and requested him to prepare an affidavit for Mrs. Thayer to make relative to Pattmore's guilt. The next morning it was ready, and Mrs. Thayer swore to the facts as therein set forth. I then told the Captain to remain in Chicago until I should send for him, and that evening I took the train for Greenville.

On my arrival there I called on Dr. Stuart and learned that his analysis had been finished that day. He had found enough poison in Mrs. Pattmore's bowels to make it certain that she had died from that cause, and not from natural disease. I then made an affidavit, charging Pattmore with murder, and I also filed Mrs. Thayer's affidavit in the court. Everything was done quietly, so that Pattmore was arrested before any one except the sheriff and the judge knew that a warrant had been issued. The arrest created immense excitement; a bitter political campaign was in progress, and it was charged, as before, that the arrest was made for political effect. The grand jury was in session, however, and I sent for Captain Sumner and Mrs. Thayer at once. The testimony of Mrs. Thayer, the nurse, and the grave-diggers, made a pretty strong case; but when I clinched the whole matter with the testimony of Dr. Stuart, there was no longer any doubt in the minds of the jury as to Pattmore's guilt. He was immediately indicted for murder in the first degree, and was consigned to prison to await trial.

The trial took place very soon afterward, and the lawyers for the defense made a very strong fight to clear their client. They were successful to the extent of saving him from execution, but he was sentenced to a term of ten years in the penitentiary.

CHAPTER XI.

SOME years after Pattmore was sentenced, I was walking down Broadway, New York, when I happened to meet Captain Sumner. Our greetings were very cordial, and I invited him to visit me at my New York office.

"I shall be very glad, indeed, to come," he said; "I often think of you, and I can never forget how much I am indebted to you. By the way, I should like to bring a friend with me."

"Do so, by all means," I replied; "I shall always be glad to see any of your friends. But how is Mrs. Thayer? Do you intend to bring her to see me?"

"No; she is not in this country now," he answered, with a pleasant smile; "but she was in good health when I last heard from her, and was very happy, indeed. Henry Thayer returned to the United States about a month after we had settled down on my farm, and he immediately came to see me. I need not tell you how delighted he was to find Annie waiting for him. Their old love for each other returned with redoubled power, and now nothing could separate them. When Annie began to speak of her past follies and errors, Henry stopped her instantly: 'No, Annie,' he said, 'let the dead bury the dead — we will live for the future. Our past shall be forgotten except such memories as are pleasant.' They have resided for several years in China, where Henry is a partner in a wealthy firm. They have two lovely children, and life runs very smoothly and pleasantly for them. I know that this great change in her life was largely due to you, Mr. Pinkerton, and I shall never cease to be grateful for your exertions to save her from misery. I owe you still another debt, which I will tell you about to-morrow, when I bring my friend to see you."

"I am very glad to know that Mrs. Thayer is so happy," I said; "give my regards to her when you write. I must hurry on now, Captain, as I have an important engagement; so good-bye. Bring your friend any time to-morrow afternoon."

So saying, I shook his hand and passed on. The next day he came sailing in, with a fine looking lady of middle age leaning contentedly on his arm.

"Mr. Pinkerton," said the Captain, with a very complacent expression, "I'm spliced. Allow me to introduce Mrs. Sumner—lately Mrs. Agnew."

THE END.

ALSO AVAILABLE

Pinkerton travels to Atkinson, Mississippi, to investigate the murder of bank teller George Gordon and the theft of more than $130,000 in the City Bank of Atkinson. Atkinson appears at first to be no more than a quiet town of shopkeepers, laborers, and businessmen. But dark secrets lurk beneath the town's Southern facade, and Pinkerton wastes no time in discovering them. Traveling under the guise of a cotton speculator, Pinkerton makes inquiries into the crime without drawing suspicion.

Although George's body was discovered in the morning, he was in the habit of remaining in the bank after hours. And upon learning that George would never let anyone into the locked bank save "only one or two personal friends," Pinkerton is certain George must have known his killer! But without much hard evidence, the Scottish detective must use all of his cunning to deduce the identity of the murderous thief and extract a confession.

Paper $15.95, ISBN 978-1-60635-415-5

This collaboration with Kent State University Special Collections and Archives brings these classic books from the Borowitz Collection back in print.

"The Borowitz Collection is the greatest private true crime library ever amassed."—Laura James, attorney and true crime writer, author of *The Beauty Defense: Femmes Fatales on Trial*

BLACK SQUIRREL BOOKS®

an imprint of The Kent State University Press
www.KentStateUniversityPress.com

Upon receiving a telegram that reads, "First National Bank robbed, please come, or send at once" from Thomas Locke in Somerset, Michigan, Pinkerton sets off to investigate the crime. After journeying to the quaint town in a blizzard, the detective learns that $65,000 of treasury bonds, notes, and cash had disappeared from the bank's vault overnight. Only one man knew the combination: the bank's cashier, Mr. Norton. When Pinkerton's subsequent examination of the crime scene reveals no signs of forced entry, it starts to look like Mr. Norton committed the crime.

But if Pinkerton has learned anything during his three decades of detective work, it is that initial appearances are often deceiving, and he narrows the investigation down to three suspects close to the cashier. However, he soon discovers that the promise of exorbitant wealth can tempt even the most honorable man to commit treacherous crimes.
Paper $15.95, ISBN 978-1-60635-414-8

This collaboration with Kent State University Special Collections and Archives brings these classic books from the Borowitz Collection back in print.

"The Borowitz Collection is the greatest private true crime library ever amassed."—Laura James, attorney and true crime writer, author of *The Beauty Defense: Femmes Fatales on Trial*